STOLEN MAGIC

MARINA FINLAYSON

FINESSE SOLUTIONS

Cover design by Karri Klawiter
Model stock image from Taria Reed/The Reed Files
Editing by Larks & Katydids
Formatting by Polgarus Studio

Published by Finesse Solutions Pty Ltd
2016/10/#01

Author's note: This book was written and produced in Australia and uses British/Australian spelling conventions, such as "colour" instead of "color", and "-ise" endings instead of "-ize" on words like "realise".

Finlayson, Marina, author.
Stolen magic / Marina Finlayson.
ISBN 9780994239174 (paperback)
Finlayson, Marina. Shadows of the Immortals; bk. 1.
Fantasy fiction.

For Malcolm, who makes it all possible.
I love you with broccoli on top.

1

The rain made the rooftop slippery, but it also meant people were even less likely to look up and see me crouched there. Shifters looked up—particularly if their animal form was a bird—but shifters were hunters, and alertness came with the territory. Humans had mostly forgotten they were prey, and had lost the awareness of their environment that had once kept them from becoming some predator's dinner. Fortunately for me. Even the drunkest observer would have found something fishy about a woman dressed head to toe in black, surrounded by a small army of cats.

Rain trickled down my neck, icy fingers on my bare skin. The cats waited patiently, as only hunters can, their life force glowing softly to my inner sight. The connections between us also glowed, strands of light snaking out from me as if some kid had been waving a sparkler through the damp air. Wet fur pressed against me on all sides as I crouched on the rooftop, watching the last stragglers from the pub stagger home in the rain. It was spring in beautiful downtown Berkley's Bay—*best holiday destination on the south coast!!*, as the sign on the road into town proudly proclaimed—but the cold rain fell regardless, and the staggerers would be only too glad to get out from under their dripping umbrellas and into their warm homes.

From up here I had a bird's-eye view of the small harbour. Like protective arms, the breakwaters encircled the tiny fishing fleet and the handful of tourist boats rocking gently on the dark water. On shore, the buildings huddled together against the winds that roared in off the sea in winter, their roofs zigging and zagging down the street all the way to the mayor's imposing residence at the end. Ocean frontage. The biggest house in town, apart from Councillor Steele's up on the headland. Nothing but the best for the shapers.

Mayor Johnson's lights had gone out some time ago, but I shared the cats' predatory patience. I waited on the wet roof until the house had been dark a good half-hour.

"Time to go, ladies and gents."

Nine pairs of yellow eyes glinted at me in the light from the streetlamps. Nine sleek wet bodies rose and paced the rooftops with me. I crouched low out of habit, but there was no one to see as we flowed from one roof to the next along the row. My foot skidded out from under me once, bringing my heart leaping into my mouth, but on the whole my borrowed agility kept me on my feet despite the slipperiness of the wet tiles.

Nine was probably overkill, but the number appealed to me. Nine cats, nine lives. Not that they could lend me their lives, but their abilities came with the link I'd forged when I'd called them to me earlier. Cats were useful for their night vision and their seemingly effortless leaping and climbing. In view of the weather, I figured the more agility the better.

At the end of the row of terrace houses, a laneway cut between the terraces and the Mayor's home. His house stood a storey higher than the surrounding homes, which gave me easy access into the upper-storey windows, as long as I made the jump across the laneway in one piece. It was only a couple of metres. Piece of cake.

I leapt, and caught the windowsill with both hands, my booted feet scrabbling for purchase against the wet bricks. Two tabbies made the leap as well, landing neatly on the sill. I shooed them out of the way and hauled myself up. Very thoughtful of the local architects to start a fashion for such wide windowsills.

The window wasn't locked. That was a nice local custom, too. No one in Berkley's Bay locked their upper-storey windows, as if it were only city thieves who could climb, and the local ones would be content with ground-floor breaking and entering. Not that I was complaining.

Thanks to the cats, my night vision was boosted far beyond its normal range. I was in a bedroom, though it had the impersonal feel of a guest room. Nothing sat on top of the small chest of drawers by the bed—no books, knickknacks, or other personal effects—and there was a musty smell in the room that suggested no one had slept in the bed for some time. The two tabbies padded across the room after me as I headed for the door.

I cracked it open and peeked out, the cats brushing past my ankles. The faint sound of snoring drifted from behind a door further along the hall. That would be the mayor's bedroom, then. I headed the other way, towards the stairs that would take me down to the lower level. That was where the shrine would be.

My two feline shadows stuck close to my heels as I slunk down the stairs, stepping on the outside of each tread, where it was less likely to creak. The mayor was only a minor power, a water prime with a weak earth secondary, so his house wasn't as grand as some I'd seen, but it was pretty swish by local standards. Berkley's Bay was a holiday town. Most of the houses looked like they'd been constructed on the cheap, with bits added on here and there as afterthoughts, or as the families that owned them had grown. Kind of like the human territories, actually. It reminded me more of the town I'd grown up in than any shaper town I'd seen.

Downstairs, polished cedar floorboards gleamed in the silvery light spilling from the semicircle of glass above the front door. A large lounge room opened off the foyer on one side. On the other, a closed door looked more promising. The cats lost interest in what I was doing and slipped away as I opened it. I loosened my grip on their minds, letting them wander. I didn't need them for this part.

And bingo. Here was Mayor Johnson's shrine, to the water god that had given him his powers. Or so the shaper myths said. People who followed the One True God—humans, mostly—said He'd created the shapers, same as everything else. That they were no more special than cockroaches or mosquitoes, and just as annoying. To absolutely no one's surprise, the shapers' preferred mythology put themselves centre stage, the children of a race of divine beings who gave them the earth as their plaything and then conveniently disappeared.

No one could actually agree on who those divine beings, known as the First Shapers, were. Some said the Norse gods, some the Greek or Roman, while others called on Celtic mythology, or Indian, or Chinese. Every culture had gods who fit the bill in its pantheon. Naturally, there'd been wars fought over the details—shapers could get just as crazy over religion as humans—but, at least on this continent, most shapers had agreed to disagree. New Holland was actually pretty progressive, if even half of what I'd heard about the Old World was true. In parts of Europa, worshipping at the wrong altar was still a hanging offence.

I shut the door of the shrine behind me. There sure was a lot of gold on that statue. Not that that mattered. I wasn't taking it for its resale value.

"Manannan Mac Lir," I whispered. "Mayor Johnson is a rebel. Who'd have thought?"

The Greek gods were in fashion in these parts. I bet Johnson having a statue of the Irish god of the sea in his shrine, instead of Poseidon, would raise a few eyebrows if the Sapphire Council heard about it. Almost made me want to tell them.

Ha. That would be the day, when I voluntarily got into a conversation with a shaper.

The statue was the size of my head, and made a hefty weight in my hand—just not as heavy as it should have if it really was made of gold. Looked like Johnson wasn't *that* fond of old Manannan. I tucked it into my backpack anyway, grinning as I pictured the Mayor's confusion the next time he came to pray, and discovered the god had abandoned him. It would serve him right.

A cat yowled somewhere in the dark house. My heart lurched, and I jumped so hard I nearly dropped the backpack on my foot. Quickly I reached out, searching for the tabbies who'd come with me. I'd been so preoccupied with Johnson's statue that I'd lost track of what the cats were up to.

Bad move. One of them had caught a mouse. The yowl had been its way of telling the world what a fearsome hunter it was. I froze with my hand on the doorknob, listening. Stillness lay on the house. Not even the sound of Johnson's snoring could be heard.

Oh, shit. A light flicked on upstairs. Johnson was awake.

What the hell are you doing? You didn't go to the pub!

I jumped, even though I recognised Syl's voice, and I knew it had only sounded in my head.

Syl was my constant companion, and I nearly always had a link open to her so that we could chat. It was my peculiar gift, this ability to link with animals. It wasn't shaping—I certainly couldn't hurl fireballs or drain rivers or do any of the other impressive shit with the five elements that shapers indulged in. It was just something I could do, and as far as I'd ever been able to discover, I was the only person who could do it. Not that I told anyone about it anymore. I'd learned my lesson a long time ago.

Not a good time, Syl, I sent back to her, mind to mind. Last I'd seen, she'd been curled up in the middle of her bed, her elegant body a neat circle, tail tucked under her chin. She'd opened one jade-green eye momentarily as I left, but shut it again without comment. Of course, I hadn't changed into my working clothes until I was out of her sight.

I can tell that. Her mental voice was as acidic as her real one, though it had been months since I'd heard it, months since she'd taken human form. *_Whatever you're doing, you just got such a shock I nearly fell off the bed. Where are you?_*

A world of suspicion attached to those three little words. I hesitated, giving the tabbies I'd brought with me a mental shove towards the window by which we'd entered.

It wasn't a shock. _Just a little jolt of adrenaline._

Fortunately, our link didn't allow Syl to see through my eyes, though I could use her senses if I wished. I'd known she wouldn't approve of tonight's excursion, hence the sneaking off without her.

My heart sped up as I thrust my awareness out through the dark house. I found the dead mouse's brothers and sisters lurking inside the walls in the kitchen, and brought them out, skittering across the floor to be my spies. Even better, one of the family was upstairs already. Perhaps it and the one the cat had caught had been up there together, mountaineering, or whatever mice do for kicks. Gently I guided the little spark of life into the hallway, checking on the mayor.

He stood in the doorway of his bedroom, his long

shadow stretching across the floor in front of him, outlined by the light spilling from the room behind him. From a mouse's perspective, he looked enormous and threatening. He'd probably look pretty threatening from a burglar's perspective, too, but it was too late now to consider that even a weak watershaper was plenty strong enough to make short work of a mere human. Particularly with the whole damn ocean right outside his house. Shaper tsunamis had wiped out entire towns before. Best to get out of here before he got much closer.

It's one o'clock in the morning, Lexi. What are you doing?

I eased the door to the shrine open just far enough and slipped through the gap, my backpack a heavy weight on my shoulders. The front door was only a few steps across the foyer.

Heading for the mayor's front door, I said truthfully.

At this time of night? I doubt he'll appreciate a visit. Wait … A complex whirl of emotion swept across our link: fear, anger, and worry mixed with a deep resignation. We'd only met a year ago, but she knew me better than anyone. *_Which side of the door are you on?_*

The wrong one.

Upstairs, the mouse shrank back into a doorway as the mayor moved. A click flooded the hallway with light that spilled down the stairs. Time to go. I closed the distance between me and the front door in three steps—the mayor's heavy tread sounded on the carpeted floor above, and I had to be out of here before he caught sight of me.

You're in the mayor's house? _What is_ wrong _with you? We're supposed to be hiding out here. Keeping our heads down. How is breaking and entering laying low?_

I was only half listening to her, my attention focused on the sounds from upstairs, my shoulders hunched in anticipation of a blow. Dammit, I should have watched those cats or, better yet, made them stay outside. I'd been doing this long enough to know better. Nine months on the big city streets of Crosston had made me quite an accomplished thief.

My hand closed on the door handle, but when I tried to turn it, it wouldn't budge. Deadlocked. Why did the mayor have to be so goddamned untrusting? What did a shaper have to fear? The man was a watershaper, with the power to move the seas if he ever chose to get off his fat arse. Or perhaps not. A truly powerful watershaper probably wouldn't be content to live as the mayor of a tinpot little town like Berkley's Bay, and one in the heart of fireshaper territory, no less. The Ruby Council held sway here, and the Sapphire Council's seat of power was a long way away.

Heart pounding, I glanced over my shoulder. In a moment, Johnson would reach the top of the stairs. I'd be caught. And I had no defence against a watershaper's powers.

I sprinted for the lounge room, uncaring of the noise I made. But the foyer was wide, and a blast of water as powerful as a fire hose caught me halfway across, knocking me from my feet. I slid across the floor in a spray of icy water and slammed into the wall.

The mayor stood at the top of the stairs, his face red, bellowing something that I couldn't hear over the roar of the water. I tried to get up, but the force of the water held me pinned, each drop an icy nail that hammered into my skin. So maybe he *was* only a second-rate watershaper, but he was good enough to drown me. Turning my face away from the deluge, I gasped for breath.

Then I took the only option left to me, and prodded the little mouse into action.

A very unmasculine shriek rose above the thunder of the water as the mouse faithfully skittered along the hallway and clawed its way up the mayor's pyjama leg. The jet of water stopped abruptly. Soaking wet, I scrambled to my feet and darted into the shadows of the lounge room. I heaved a window open, to the heavy thumping of the mayor dancing a jig at the top of the stairs, complete with slapping sounds and little cries of horror.

The smell of rain lingered on the cool night air, but I sucked great lungfuls of it gratefully. I half-clambered, half-fell over the windowsill in a squelch of wet clothes and shivering limbs. Safe outside, I released the mouse, who leapt free and bolted for cover, its tiny heart beating almost as wildly as my own. I followed suit, disappearing into the shadows behind the mayor's house. Now I was grateful for the change of clothes in my pack. I couldn't stop shaking. That water had felt like it was sourced straight from the bloody Antarctic. I needed to peel myself out of these wet clothes, but the first priority was putting a little more room between me and the enraged mayor. I hitched the backpack into a more comfortable position and turned away from the lights.

I'll be home soon. I jogged along the laneway, teeth chattering, keeping to the shadows. Not that there was anyone to see me. I cast my senses wide, and nothing bigger than a cat lurked in the darkness around me. A cool salt breeze blew in off the sea, teasing at my dark hair in its dripping ponytail, and I shivered some more. **Nothing to worry about now.**

Maybe not* now.* Syl's mental voice was grumpy. **What about when he misses whatever you took? I assume you took something?

You make me sound like a kleptomaniac. This is the first job I've done since we left Crosston.

For good reason, she pointed out. **Did you also want to put up a big flashing sign saying* Here we are *in case Anders misses the hints you've so thoughtfully laid out for him?**

**Relax. Anders is a fireshaper, Johnson's a watershaper.*

_They probably don't even know each other. How is Anders going to find out Johnson's lost his altarpiece? And even if he does, there's no reason for him to connect it to us._*

You took his altarpiece? He's going to kill you! She almost moaned. *_Why would you do a thing like that?_*

He deserves it, I said. Even more so now that he'd blasted me with ice water. My feet crunched on gravel as I left the paved street and started up the road to the clifftop. *_He fired Holly today._*

So? She's leaving to have the baby soon anyway.

Yeah, but she needs a job to come back to. Joe doesn't make enough to support them both without her salary. Joe and Holly lived in the apartment across the landing from mine, and we'd been friends since they'd turned up with wine and chocolate on the night I moved in. They were my kind of people, even though they were both werewolves. Thinking about the hardship that Johnson's arbitrary decision would cause them brought my resentment boiling back.

And how does stealing Johnson's altarpiece help? The first person you try and sell that to is going to turn you in.

I sighed. She was just scared—so scared that she hadn't left her cat shape in the months we'd been here in Berkley's Bay. If she'd given herself time to think about it, she would surely have realised I wasn't that stupid. This was the fear talking.

I'm not going to try to sell it. I was breathing deeply now of the salt air as I climbed the path, sure-footed in the dark. At least the exercise had warmed me enough that I'd stopped shivering, though my wet clothes clung uncomfortably. The only sound out here, other than my feet squelching in my sodden shoes, was the waves breaking on the rocks at the base of the cliff. I stopped partway up and looked back over the lights below. Most of the houses were dark, but the streetlights cast a soft glow over the sleeping town. I grinned as I saw that every light in Johnson's house was ablaze. Perhaps the mayor would be awake all night, frightened that a mouse might leap from nowhere to scale the vast bulk of his pyjama-clad leg.

Then what* are *you going to do with it? Syl's mental tone was a little calmer now. **Why risk exposing us to take it?**

To seaward all was dark, though my night vision, enhanced by the link to Syl's cat form, revealed the occasional flash of white down below as a wave broke. I reached the top of the cliff, and stepped as close as I dared to the edge, a salty wind in my face.

If I'd kept going along the clifftop path, I would have come to the home of another shaper, one far more powerful than the mouse-fearing mayor. But I wasn't afraid of running afoul of Jake Steele, because this home, despite being by far the grandest house in town, was only a holiday house. And Steele spent all his time in the city. He had a seat on the Ruby Council, and not just as one of the Seated, but as a full Master, making him far too grand and important to spend any time in a tiny little one-horse town like Berkley's Bay. Most of his time would be spent either in Crosston or in his regional capital, overseeing the whole of the South-East. His "holiday house" here in Berkley's Bay commanded three-hundred-and-sixty-degree views from its spot on top of the headland, but I kept well away from its manicured lawns. Hidden by the dark trees, I pulled the statue of Manannan Mac Lir from my backpack.

I wound my arm back, the statue snug in my hand. *_I'm going to hide it somewhere he'll never find it._*

The golden sea god arced through the sky, tumbling end over end, and disappeared into the night. I didn't even hear a splash over the relentless shushing of the waves below. The irony of it appealed to my warped sense of humour. If only he knew where it was, a watershaper like Johnson could easily retrieve it.

Syl's mental voice was plaintive. *_But_ why?*

Did she really need to ask, after what the fireshaper Anders had done to us? *_Someone's gotta stick it to these shaper bastards. Sack a pregnant woman for no reason? They think they can do whatever they like, just because they're shapers._*

They can, _Lexi. That's the point. If you couldn't accept that, you should've stayed in the human territories._

Let Johnson see what it's like to have random shit happen to him _for a change. Karma's a bitch._

You're going to get us killed.

You worry too much.

And you don't worry enough.

2

It was just on closing time the next night, and still pouring, when my carefully constructed life began to unravel. It only takes a little tug to loosen one thread and then, before you know it, you're missing a whole sleeve, and the remains of your shirt are trailing behind you in the dirt.

A customer—probably my last customer of the evening, considering the weather—had just left the shop. Caught by the wind, the door slammed shut behind him, shaking the glass panes in their panels; the bell above the door jingled a complaint at the rough treatment. The cold wind took the opportunity to fling itself around the front of the store, whooshing past the books piled on the sale table, across the biography shelves and the thrillers and crime novels that faced the door. It ruffled Syl's fur where she lay curled on a faded pink cushion, in pride of place on the battered counter beside the clunky old cash register. She flicked one ear in disapproval and yawned widely, showing her pink tongue and needle-sharp teeth.

**I feel like vegetarian pizza tonight,* * she said.

“It’s a shame cats are obligate carnivores, then,” I said. “If you took your human form now and then, you could eat all the vegetarian food your little feline heart craved.”

I could link with any animal at all, but I couldn’t talk to them the way I talked to Syl, because Syl wasn’t exactly an animal. My friend was a werecat, who’d shifted into cat form when we’d left the city three months ago and had refused to budge out of it ever since, despite my pleas. She’d been a cat so long and so determinedly that no one in Berkley’s Bay had seen her human form. Not even the other shifters in town realised she was more than a cat. No one did, except maybe Alberto.

Alberto owned the town’s only pub, plus this tiny second-hand bookshop and half the other businesses in town. He’d been in Berkley’s Bay so long he was practically an institution, and if there was anything worth knowing going on in his town, you could be sure Alberto Alinari would know about it.

**I like being a cat.* * She stretched luxuriously, her front legs straight and stiff, the pads of her feet separated and her claws extended. She pricked at the velvet cushion with those claws, kneading it into a more pleasing shape.

“Don’t you ruin that cushion. I’m not buying you another one.”

Cheapskate.

I checked the old clock on the wall above historical fiction. Its elaborate filigree hands showed five minutes past six. Alberto was a little late tonight. He usually popped over once it got dark, to see how the bookshop was doing. That was why I stayed open after the other shops in our little row closed. Syl and I rented the apartment above the shop; it was dirt cheap, and the commute to work was easy, so I didn't mind staying open later. And since Alberto provided the accommodation as well as the job, it only seemed fair.

Besides, my mother had brought me up to be polite to vampires.

They occupied a unique place among shifters. They were rarely seen in their shifted form. Maybe being a bat wasn't much fun, or perhaps the fact that they had to spend the daylight hours asleep made them reluctant to give up any of their human nightlife to flying around hunting insects. Most people forgot they were shifters at all, and once the "undead" rumours got started they seemed to be in a class of their own. But I'd seen Alberto breathing. I figured the undead thing was just something they cultivated to add to their mystique.

I knelt on the worn carpet in front of the romance section. A lady had been in here earlier today, rummaging around, pulling things off the shelf and then shoving them back every which way. People, even booklovers, just didn't have the same respect for second-hand books as they did for new ones. I'd been too busy to re-sort the books earlier, so I took the opportunity now to get them back into alphabetical order. While I was doing that the door jingled its discordant tune and I felt another gust of icy wind.

Hunk alert! Hunk alert! Syl called from the front counter.

I scrambled up as the most gorgeous man I'd ever seen rounded the shelves. He was tall—way taller than me, which was saying something, since I towered over most women. I looked up, past a wide muscular chest and a broad pair of shoulders, to a face with cheekbones so chiselled you could have cut yourself on them. Above that was a pair of blue eyes that would have been striking if not for the hint of arrogance in their cool gaze. Damn. That was shaper arrogance. My interest cooled as fast as if someone had poured a bucket of ice-cold water over me.

"Can I help you?" No man had the right to look that hot, especially not a shaper. As if they didn't have enough advantages already over us lesser folk.

Those arrogant eyes flicked over me. "I was looking for Alberto. Is he here?"

"No." Shapers were trouble, even ones that looked criminally good in jeans and tight T-shirts. "Did you ask at the pub?"

Berkley's Bay wasn't a big place. Its numbers swelled in

summer when the tourists arrived, but at this time of year it was only the locals, and every second house stood empty. The pub was where everyone congregated, the heart of the little beachside community. It had no windows, and there had never been a break-in there, since everyone knew that the owner slept the day away in the cellar. Alberto was a convivial host; wine and beer flowed until late on Friday and Saturday nights. He could almost always be found propping up the bar after dark.

"I went there first. They told me to look here," he said, as if that should have been obvious.

"Right." So I was just supposed to produce the vampire out of thin air? Did I look like a magician?

"I'll wait."

Lucky me. Well, at least the view was good, though he seemed oddly hostile, considering we'd just met. As if it was my fault Alberto hadn't appeared on demand.

Nice arse, said Syl.

My thoughts exactly. Not that I would tell her that. And not that either of us could afford to be distracted. *_Sylvie Wentworth! Behave yourself._*

What? I'm just saying. Nothing wrong with admiring the view, is there?

He's a shaper.

Damn. Well, wouldn't that rot your socks. Despite her flippant tone, she leapt down from the counter and disappeared behind the shelves. I didn't blame her for wanting to put some distance between her and the shaper. Our experiences with them so far hadn't been happy ones.

I stayed with the romances as long as I could, hoping that Alberto would appear and take my unwelcome visitor away, but eventually I had to admit they were all in perfect alphabetical order. I loved this place; it had that old-book smell of paper and dreams, and on a sunny day the honey-coloured wood of the shelves glowed in the light that crept in the front windows and through the panes of glass set into the bright red door. Every day when I unlocked that door and flipped the sign from CLOSED to OPEN I took a deep breath of that intoxicating smell, and wondered what treasures might come through the door today, their covers worn smooth from years of love.

Tonight's customer stood in front of the historical fiction section, his back to me, while the rain pounded down outside. Having him in my little bookshop haven set my teeth on edge. Shapers were unpredictable, liable to take what they wanted without regard for the rights or property of non-shapers. Thank the gods there were so few of them, or the world would be in an even bigger mess than it already was, divided into human territories and shaper lands, rubbing along in an uneasy peace that always threatened to spill over into another outright war. Personally, if I never met another shaper in my life it would be too soon.

I slid behind the high wooden counter and glared at his broad shoulders. What was a shaper doing in a tiny little no-account place like Berkley's Bay? As far as I was concerned, shapers were always bad news. I busied myself with tidying the already tidy counter, rearranging the displays of bookmarks and other knickknacks, wishing that he and his cute arse would take themselves elsewhere.

When I looked up, he was watching me.

"What?" I demanded. "Have I got a smudge on my face?"

"You look beautiful, as I'm sure you're well aware. What's your name?"

I was *well aware*? What was that supposed to mean? Was he calling me vain?

"Lexi," I said shortly. If I was vain, why was I wearing jeans and a windcheater, now dusty from the new arrivals I'd sorted this morning? I had no lipstick on—no makeup at all, in fact—and my long black hair was pulled back in a simple ponytail. I was certainly not *vain*. Nor did his opinion matter one bit.

"Lexi," he repeated, his expression cool. "I'm Jacob Steele."

Uh-oh, said Syl. **The lord high mucky-muck?* That *Jacob Steele?**

I doubt there's more than one. My heart sank. Even more reason to keep a low profile: Jacob Steele was one of the four Masters on the Ruby Council, second only to the Ruby Adept himself. The whole of the South-East fell under his jurisdiction. Despite his owning that empty mansion on the clifftop, I'd never expected to see him here. He was way too important for a place like Berkley's Bay. This guy who looked as though he'd stepped off the cover of one of our romance novels was one of the most powerful shapers on the eastern seaboard. An anxious hollow opened in the pit of my stomach.

The way he was staring at me made me nervous. Well, more nervous. It was not a pleasant look. I cast a desperate glance out at the rainy night. Where was Alberto?

"I'm curious, Lexi." He folded his arms across his chest. Despite the cold, he wore no jacket, and without meaning to, I found my eye drawn like a magnet to the tanned biceps his T-shirt showed. "What are you?"

Suddenly chilled, I jerked my gaze up to his face and met cold blue eyes. "What do you mean?"

"There are basically three kinds of people in the world: shapers, shifters, and sheep. You're not a shifter, and you're certainly not a shaper, but you don't feel like a sheep either. So what are you?"

He forgot Number 4: shitheads, Syl said acidly.

Not the time, Syl. The last thing I needed was another shaper trying to poke his nose into my business. I squared my shoulders. I wouldn't let him see how much that chill gaze frightened me. "I don't know what you're talking about."

"Oh, I think you do." He flexed his fingers, and tiny flames sprang to life on their tips. I didn't quite manage to hide my flinch. Hard blue eyes pinned me to the spot. "There's something different about you. Tell me what you are."

The flames danced a little higher. I swallowed hard. He could kill me in an instant, just for kicks, or for no reason at all, and there was nothing anyone could do to stop him. The hairs on my arms rose as a chill ran down my spine.

"You might want to go easy on the fire show." My voice came out in a frightened squeak, but I refused to be cowed. Damn fireshapers ought to be put down like the savages they were. I clenched my fists to hide their shaking. "This shop belongs to Alberto. I don't think he'll be too impressed if his stock goes up in flames, but it's your funeral, I guess."

He moved closer, and I stood my ground, just barely. My cool act probably wasn't fooling him, but I was saved by the bell—literally. The door flew open, setting the bell to jangling wildly, and a man I'd never seen before rushed inside in a swirl of wind and spattered raindrops.

"Sir, you're needed," he said, without even glancing at me. Steele let the flames wink out, and I remembered to breathe again. "Someone's reported a missing child. Mr Alinari is organising a search party."

Without a word, the shaper strode out into the night.

3

Syl came out from behind the bookshelves, her tail still flicking from side to side in agitation.

What was* his *problem? Was he seriously going to set fire to the shop?

History was repeating all over again. I could smell the smoke, hear the screams. If the gods had had to invent shapers, couldn't they have come up with something big and dangerous and hungry that liked to eat them, too? I *hated* the fact that I was still shaking from his casual threats. That he felt entitled to make them.

"Shaper arsehole. They're all the same. Think they only have to snap their fingers and everyone around them will jump."

People like him were the reason Syl hadn't left her cat shape in three months. Her memories were every bit as horrifying as my own. I changed the subject to something safer.

"I wonder who's missing?"

Probably just some kid who forgot to tell his mum he was going to a friend's house after school. All a big fuss about nothing.

"Probably."

Outside the rain was still falling, not heavy but persistent, the kind of rain that seeps right through your clothes and down into your shoes until every part of you is cold, wet, and miserable. And spring had only just started, so we weren't exactly talking heat wave temperatures either.

Her tail gave one final nervous twitch. **Maybe we should go check, just in case.**

Yeah, maybe we should. The less I saw of Jake bloody Steele the happier I'd be, but if someone's kid was missing in this weather, I couldn't hide in the shop. I took a deep breath and forced my panicked heartbeat to slow. He wasn't going to kill me if I went out there.

A few more cars than usual were parked outside the pub; people were starting to gather. Two women darted across the road, sharing one inadequate umbrella, and went inside. One was Tegan, the weretiger who ran the hair salon next door. She had her arm wrapped firmly around the smaller woman's shoulders. With a sinking heart I recognised Rosie, with a hanky clutched in one hand.

"Oh, no. I think it's Cody."

Cody was a good kid, twelve years old, with a shock of

blonde hair and a lively curiosity that sometimes led him into trouble. He was the son of Rosie and my next door neighbour Joe, though they'd split up years ago, not long after Cody had been born. Relationships between shifters and humans were often rocky, and theirs had been no exception. Since Rosie was human, Cody was too; this would have disappointed most twelve-year-olds, but Cody took it with his usual unruffled calm. Joe's pack couldn't have adored him more if he *had* been a wolf.

Syl stalked along the counter to give herself a better view of the street. **Was that Rosie that just went into the pub?*

I nodded. Rosie was a single mum again, having split with Cody's stepdad a couple of years ago. She had a job as a doctor's receptionist in the next town, and if surgery ran late, as it often did, Cody looked after himself until she got home.

Often that involved dropping into the bookshop and talking my ear off about his latest craze. He'd been in last week, looking for some information on owls, and I'd helped him find a book on birds. Let him have it for half-price, too. There wasn't much money to spare in that family, even with the little bit of support that Joe contributed. And with Holly losing her job, and the new baby on the way, that contribution would soon be even less. Damn that prat Johnson.

Damn all shapers. There were so few of them, compared

to the number of humans in the world, yet they held the balance of power. Sure, in some of the bigger human-controlled areas, like Brittania, a human might pass their whole life without ever seeing a shaper. Not so here in New Holland, unfortunately. Hell, I'd heard that in some places they didn't even have *shifters*, but that seemed too weird to be true. Shifters were far more numerous than the element-wielding shapers, though humans still outnumbered them.

"I should go help." Had Cody been taken? Surely not. Things like that just didn't happen in sleepy Berkley's Bay. Wandered off, then? That seemed almost as unlikely. Cody knew the drill: straight home after school, or to Joe and Holly's place if it was their night to have him. Apart from his visits to the bookshop, he wasn't the type to wander. But, either way, I could help.

The wolves will sniff him out, Syl said, watching another couple of cars pull up outside the pub.

Had Joe heard yet? He had a soft spot bigger than the great outdoors for that boy. "On a night like this? If there was a trail, it will have washed away by now."

She didn't reply. Syl never admitted I was right if she could possibly help it—but I *was* right. Not even Joe's nose could follow a trail in this weather.

That Steele jerk is there, she pointed out after a long pause.

"What's he going to do? Set fire to something?" Fat lot

of help that would be. "Come on. It's Cody. I've got to go over there."

Syl followed me out into the rain, though she scooted into the doorway to our apartment so fast her paws barely touched the wet pavement. She waited there while I locked the shop, then led the way up the stairs to the landing, her tail waving above her back like a black flag.

Two doors faced each other across the landing. Number 1 belonged to Joe and Holly, but they wouldn't be home with Cody missing.

I unlocked the door of Number 2 and followed Syl inside, flicking lights on as I went. It wasn't a very big apartment; though Alberto had called it "two bedrooms", the second bedroom had been designed for a dwarf. It was just as well Syl preferred her cat form for now, or it might have made her claustrophobic. The larger bedroom was mine, and we shared the cramped bathroom, which also housed the washing machine and dryer. The kitchen was small but adequate, but the best thing about the apartment was the view from the living room, which looked back across a row of single-storey houses to a view of the bay. At the moment that view was dark and shrouded with rain, but I was looking forward to spending summer evenings on the balcony enjoying the breeze and watching the colours of the sea and sky change.

I put on hiking boots and a waterproof jacket and grabbed the flashlight from under the kitchen sink.

"Back as soon as I can."

Let me know how it goes.

I hurried down the stairs and out into the rain, pulling my jacket tighter around me as I dashed across the road to the pub. Alberto arrived at the same time, wearing a black polo shirt and black trousers. In three months, I'd never seen him wear anything else. The only variation was in the thickness of the fabric. In winter he'd worn wool; now that spring was here he'd switched to a lighter cotton. He always looked immaculate, and kept his bar the same way.

He held the door open for me and we entered the "airlock", a small dark space before another door opened into the noise and light of the pub itself. The double doors helped keep out the hated sunlight, though Alberto spent most of the day sleeping in the extensive cellars beneath the pub.

"After you," he murmured.

I pushed open the inner door and found a hive of industry. The pub was one of the oldest buildings in town, and was furnished in old-fashioned style, its warm wooden tables lit by low-hanging pendant lights that shed a rosy glow over the scene. The main bar still had some of the original features. The long wooden bar had decorative carving along the front: wattle blossom and sprays of eucalyptus leaves, oiled and polished over the years to a dark glowing brown. The tables and chairs were all new, and apparently much more comfortable than the originals, according to the regulars. Alberto had removed all the windows, but some of the original wallpaper still survived. It was green and gold and not all that attractive, but I guess it had historic value.

Someone had found a huge map of the area, and had it spread out over two tables pushed together. Jake Steele stood with a group of men around the map, the light catching blue highlights in his dark hair as he bent over it. He looked up as we entered.

"Jake!" Alberto said. "I wondered whose limo that was outside."

Steele crossed the floor and shook the vampire's hand. "I've only just arrived in town. I stopped by to see you, and then this happened ..." He waved a hand at the chaos around us.

I left the two men and headed over to where Rosie sat on a barstool next to Tegan.

"Is it Cody?" I said under my breath to Tegan. She was a weretiger; she had excellent hearing.

She nodded. Outwardly her face was as calm as ever, but her tawny eyes were worried. "And Jamie Hernandez. It's not like Cody," she muttered. "Any other kid and nobody would bat an eyelid, but Cody ..."

My thoughts exactly. And apparently half the town agreed, judging by the numbers that were still arriving.

Steele was splitting people into groups and assigning sections of the map to be searched.

"Hi, Rosie." I gave her a quick hug. "Don't worry, we'll find him. I'm sure he's fine."

She gave me a tremulous smile. Rosie looked tired at the best of times, but now she looked exhausted. The skin around her eyes was pink, as if she'd been crying, but there were no tears now.

"He was supposed to be at Jamie's place," she said. "I stopped there on my way home from work to pick him up, but Michelle said Jamie had told her they were going to *my* place. I don't understand. It's not like Cody to lie."

I nodded sympathetically. "But at least that means they're together, wherever they are." And probably ruled out that they'd been snatched by someone. One boy, yes, but two boys? Pretty unlikely. "Where's Joe?"

"He's gone to see if he can find a trail," Tegan said. Her shrug added that she thought there was no chance of that, but Joe wasn't the type to sit still when his son was missing.

I glanced across at Steele again, his tall figure drawing my eye against my will. He and Alberto had their heads together over the map.

"Tegan and I knocked on every door between my place and Michelle's," Rosie said. "No one saw them. I'm just worried they might have gone to the beach. With the weather we've had today ..."

She trailed off. The beach was on the seaward side of the point, not sheltered like our little harbour. It was often closed in poor weather, the waves too high for safe swimming, but when had that ever stopped boys?

"It's way too cold for swimming today. Even for a kid! I'm sure you don't need to worry about that."

The door swung open again, and Joe trotted in, his yellow eyes startling against his dark fur. An expectant hush fell on the crowd, and I gave Rosie's shoulder a reassuring squeeze. Between one step and the next, the wolf shimmered and disappeared, transformed into a big, solid guy in jeans and a dark T-shirt. Judging by the scowl on his face, the news wasn't good. Alberto offered him one of the towels he used to wipe the bar to dry his wet hair.

Rosie slid off her barstool, and I went with her, eager to hear what news Joe had.

"No luck." He ran his hand through his wet hair, sweeping it out of his face. "There's been too much rain to pick up a trail. It's all been washed away. But we did find a couple of school bags down the back of Pike Park. I reckon they've gone into the bush there."

"Really?" Rosie said. That seemed to make her happy, though to my mind the bush held plenty of dangers for two inexperienced boys. Still, she could stop worrying that they'd been swept out to sea.

Joe's report was our signal to move out. Alberto stayed

behind to man the phones and send any latecomers to join us at the park. The rest of us headed off, cramming into the vehicles parked outside. Despite my best efforts to avoid Jake Steele, I ended up sandwiched between him and Joe in the back of the limo. He didn't make any more threats, but I felt his gaze resting on me.

Damned if I knew why he was so hostile. I refused to look at him, spending the whole time staring out the window instead. My mind ranged ahead to the park, flitting from heartbeat to heartbeat through the dripping trees.

Pike Park was a large playing field with a small, brightly coloured playground built off to one side. Once we arrived, Steele stuck close and made sure he was right alongside me when we split up to search, clearly determined not to let me out of his sight.

Beyond the dripping swings and the slippery dip running with water, several paths led off into the bush. This sea of green surrounded the whole town on the landward side. Berkley's Bay nestled between the sea on one side and the bush on the other. Some of that bush was public land, set aside for the use of the shifters, but a lot of it belonged to the massive estate of a certain shaper, whose magnificent mansion commanded a sweeping view of the whole bay from the top of its private hill. If you walked far enough along some of these trails, you'd end up alongside his fences.

If you left the trails, you could end up anywhere. There was a lot of land out there, a vast ocean of trackless green, enough for two boys to get lost in many times over. If they had strayed from the paths, the chances of us simply stumbling over them in the dark and the rain were small.

We spread out in a line, our flashlights faint pinpricks of light in the darkness, and began to walk, calling out as we went. The bush quickly closed in around us; I could barely see the flashlight of the person two links down the human chain, bobbing weakly through the rain. It was getting heavier. The rain muffled our voices, too, drowning them with its steady patter on the sodden ground.

I called out dutifully just the same, swinging my flashlight at the dripping undergrowth, watching the raindrops streak through its beam, but I wasn't focused on that. My attention spidered out in all directions, little tendrils creeping through the dripping bush, burrowing into every little dry hidey-hole and up into every tree, seeking out the bright points of life that twinkled in my inner sight like tiny stars.

Here I touched a small rodent, there a bird. Here a fox or feral cat, there a wild deer. There were animals all around us, and I slid into their minds, looked out of their eyes—a hundred different views of the trees stark against the clouds, of the hollows under logs and the dripping spaces underneath the bushes. Everywhere I looked, the bush was alive, but nowhere did I see two cold and frightened little boys.

My mind touched a mob of kangaroos foraging through the wet grass in a small clearing. I sent them bounding through the night, watching the trees swing dizzily past. I found a fox with two half-grown cubs, and sent them in the other direction, along the banks of a small creek that chattered noisily over its stony bed.

I stumbled, my attention only half on what my physical body was doing. Steele cast a sharp glance my way, though I couldn't imagine why. Stumbles were common in the dark bush. The ground beneath our feet was littered with rocks and sudden dips, and everyone was watching the beam of their flashlight, not looking down at their feet. The man on my left had tripped twice in the last half hour, with no particular attention from Steele.

Time was passing; my watch said nine o'clock already. We'd been out here over an hour, with no sign of the boys. Strands of wet hair straggled in my face; I brushed them back with fingers numb from the rain's relentless onslaught. The boys would be cold and frightened. We needed to find them soon.

At last, my questing mind found an owl soaring overhead, and I hitched a ride with her straight away. Her night vision was exceptional; back at the bar the men had been lamenting the fact that there were no owl shifters in town. The search might have been over already if we'd had one.

Wind rushed over her feathers as we sailed like a ghost through the weeping sky. Her belly was empty, but I only felt a little guilty about interrupting her hunt with my own—she was young and healthy, and wouldn't suffer for the delay.

On the ground, we had arrived at the creek that my foxes had passed earlier. The line paused as Steele contemplated the rushing water. Parts of it were deep, and broken branches reached out of the water at odd angles, hinting at hidden snags.

"Do you think they could have gone in?" the man to Steele's right asked. "It joins the river further down."

This close to the sea the river was salty, wide and deep, and it ran with a strong current, as if eager to be out at sea. If the boys had fallen in, already cold and wet, and been swept away, perhaps hurt in the fall …

The line contracted, other searchers moving in closer to see why we'd stopped.

"If it comes to that we can search the river," Steele said, "but let's not assume the worst. Perhaps they didn't come this way at all, or turned back at the creek."

"Might have crossed over," someone else said, a featureless voice in the dark. "It's not so deep further along."

"They might," Steele conceded, "but how far could they have gone in the time they had? We could be searching in the wrong direction entirely."

I was starting to think so, too. My animal friends had covered a lot more ground than we had, and none had seen any sign that the boys went this way. Those poor kids must be starving by now, and probably frightened, too. It was getting late, and I was tired of tramping through the wet—and *I* was equipped for it. The boys must be feeling much worse.

I sent my owl out wider, in great swooping passes through the rainy night. Through her eyes, I saw the lights of Steele's house below on their cliff overlooking the sea, and, farther back, the lights of the town. Nothing out here but darkness.

Then her sharp eyes spotted the smallest glint below, despite the fact that the moon was hidden behind fat dark clouds. I sent her down lower to investigate. The glint had a faint blue tinge.

She settled on the branch of a tall gum, swivelling her head to show me the scene. Huddled at the base of the tree were two small bodies. Thank goodness! One boy had his back propped against the trunk and one leg stuck straight out in front of him. Was that leg at a funny angle? It was hard to tell using the owl's sight.

The other boy was Cody. He held a mobile phone; the

blue glint was the light of its screen. He sighed and shoved the phone into his back pocket. There was probably no signal; service was a little patchy even in town. He looked fine, though both boys were drenched. The sooner I could get to them the better.

But how was I going to do that without it looking suspicious? The boys were nowhere near us, nowhere near anywhere that was currently being searched. I could hardly say, "Hey, guys, let's just try *this* way," and lead them back to the park and off into a random patch of bush that was nowhere near where we'd found their bags.

The men were still discussing the creek and what we should do. Ideally I didn't want any of them with me when I found the boys. I wiped rain out of my eyes and sniffed. The cold was making my nose run.

"I'm going to head back into signal range and ring Rosie," I said. "See if there's anywhere else they could have gone."

Joe eyed me impatiently, his irises golden with the need to turn wolf. His hair, dark with rain, was plastered to his head. In his haste to get out and find his son, he hadn't bothered to stop for wet weather gear.

"She would have said if there was."

"Just in case."

He made a noise of frustration that sounded a lot like a growl. Shifters often took refuge in their animal shape in stressful situations, but Joe was doing his best to stay in the more useful human form. "We don't want to have to go searching for you, too."

"I'll go with her," Steele said, taking my arm in a firm grip. "Give it another ten minutes and then bring everyone else back to the park. We'll regroup there."

Shit. How was I going to do this now, with him watching? Why did he have to be so bloody untrusting? I shook his hand off and strode off into the dripping bush before anyone else could volunteer to come, too. With a bit of luck, I could lose him in the dark.

Sadly, his long legs were more than equal to the task of keeping up with me. We arrived back at the park much faster than the outward journey.

"I've got signal here." Steele stopped, looking at me expectantly. Damn the man. Why hadn't he pulled shaper rank and stayed at the pub with Alberto? The mayor hadn't offered to join the search party.

Now I didn't know what to do. Should I pretend to call Rosie and get some new "information" that would lead me in the right direction? But that would be so easy to check. Someone would be bound to say something to Rosie, and then the whole thing would come unravelled. Just like my life was threatening to.

"I've got a hunch. I've seen some of the local kids head out this way before. Let's just give it a shot."

I glanced sidelong at him as we plunged back into the bush on a different path. That was the vaguest bit of handwavery ever, and he didn't look at all convinced. If he'd been suspicious of me before, this was only going to make it worse.

Sure enough, he raised a doubtful eyebrow. "You didn't think to mention this before? When we were discussing the search areas?"

"Slipped my mind." At least it was too dark for him to see me blush.

The rain had finally eased and, though it made me nervous to have his hostile presence at my back, I forged ahead, taking the lead so I wouldn't have to see that sceptical look any more. He moved quietly in the dark, with none of the slipping on stones and cracking of twigs that I was doing. A natural predator. But then, his attention wasn't split between his own mind and an owl's.

Even with the rain, the view from above was spectacular. She could make out every individual leaf on every tree. Every edge was crisp and sharp, and her ears caught even the faintest rustle among the grey shades of the night forest. Air currents teased at her feathers as she soared aloft.

I didn't bother calling out; I knew we were too far away yet for the boys to hear me. I let my owl guide me, and when I plunged off the faint trail Steele followed without question. Or even a biting remark.

We moved fast, and after about twenty minutes Steele said, "Did you hear that?"

"Cody?" I called. "Jamie? Are you there?"

A wild yell answered. "Over here! Over here!"

We veered in the direction of the voice, climbing a sudden steep rise. My boots slipped on wet rock as we scrambled up the slope, and then there was a thrashing in the bushes and a small wet boy appeared. I released my owl and she flew silently away.

"Lexi! You found us!"

I felt his hands. They were icy cold. I was about to strip off my jacket and wrap it around his shivering form when Steele stepped forward, nudging me out of the way.

He smiled at Cody reassuringly. "Hi. I'm Jake. I'm going to warm you up. Don't be scared, okay? It doesn't hurt."

"Okay." Cody didn't sound convinced, but he didn't move when Steele took his cold hands in his.

Warm orange light welled around their joined hands, then crept up Cody's arms, flickering like tiny flames. Cody watched their progress, his eyes huge.

"Whoa. That is *so* cool. Are you a fireshaper?"

"Yep."

As if anyone else would be wandering around out here wearing only a sodden T-shirt. That T-shirt clung to the hard planes of his chest, and I looked away hastily. The fire whispered over Cody's body, spreading across his torso and up his neck.

"Are you all right?" I asked him. "Are you hurt?"

"I'm fine," he said, though he didn't take his eyes off the tiny flames. They *were* kind of impressive, even I had to admit that. I'd never seen fireshaping used for anything constructive before. "But there's something wrong with Jamie's leg. He fell out of the tree, and I think it might be broken."

We followed him back to where Jamie sat propped at the base of the gum. His leg was most definitely broken. I flinched at the ugly shard of bone peeking out of his torn flesh. Poor little guy looked bad. He was shivering, too, and Steele laid his hands on him and performed the same shaping, so that both boys were outlined in an orange glow.

"Find a straight stick we can use as a splint." He tossed the command my way without even looking at me, all his attention on Jamie. "You'll be fine, mate. But we need to keep that leg as still as we can."

I nearly asked him what the magic word was, but I bit my lip and hunted around for a strong enough stick instead. He already seemed to have it in for me; there was no sense irritating him further. People who irritated shapers tended to have limited life spans.

"What were you two doing out here?" I asked Cody.

Steele pulled his T-shirt over his head in one fluid

movement and began tearing it into strips. Now *that* was a nice view. Water dripped from the tree overhead onto his muscular shoulders and ran down his broad chest—

Then he bent to bind the stick I gave him to Jamie's leg, and I saw his back. It was crisscrossed with the stripes of old scars. I stared, aghast. His whole back was one big mess of scar tissue. Wow. I'd have liked to meet the person capable of doing something like that to a shaper. Or, on second thought, maybe I wouldn't.

"Your mum thought you were going to Jamie's house after school." Determinedly I focused on Cody. Steele had probably deserved it anyway. Shaper bastard.

"We were." Cody looked down, as if he knew he'd done the wrong thing. "But on the way home Jamie was telling me how he'd found these baby possums in a tree out here, so we came out to have a look. But then Jamie fell out of the tree and hurt himself. I didn't know the way back without him, so I couldn't go for help, and I didn't have any phone signal, so I thought it was better to stay together and hope somebody found us."

"Good thinking," I said. "You wouldn't have done Jamie any good if you'd got lost trying to get help."

Steele hoisted Jamie carefully into his arms. "We'll take him to my house. It's the closest."

He strode into the dripping darkness beneath the trees without waiting to see if we followed him. How did he know the way? He didn't have a host of animal ears and eyes to guide him. But he seemed to be headed in the right direction.

"Here." I offered the flashlight to Cody. "You can carry this."

He took it, and together we followed that powerful, scarred back in silence all the way through the bush until we emerged onto a manicured lawn. Ahead of us, Steele's enormous house sprawled among dark gardens, the lights of its windows promising food and warmth.

There were going to be some happy people in town when we appeared. And I would be happiest of all, at not having to spend another minute in Jake Steele's company.

4

Steele's house was every bit as imposing on the inside as it had appeared from the outside. We entered from the rear, and Cody's eyes widened.

"Cool! You have a pool *inside*?"

We followed Steele past the glittering water, through an enormous kitchen and into the main area of the house. Steele laid Jamie down gently on a couch, then cast me an impatient glance.

"You're dripping all over the floor."

"Sorry."

"I'll get you a dry shirt."

"You're the one who needs a new shirt. I'm perfectly dry under this jacket." I resisted the urge to wring out my wet hair all over his carpet and pulled out my phone: four bars of coverage. "I'll just ring Alberto while you're finding some clothes."

I didn't like the guy, but I wasn't blind. He was seriously ripped, and my eyes kept straying to places they shouldn't. It was a relief when he disappeared down the hall. I gave the good news to Alberto, who said he'd send Steele's limo out for us, and the ambulance to take Jamie to the community hospital. They'd been on standby while we searched. The poor kid's face was very pale. He was warm, thanks to Steele, but obviously hurting.

"The ambulance will be here soon," I told him. "They'll give you something to help with the pain."

Sure enough, they turned up just as Steele came back in, wearing a dark blue shirt over clean jeans. Once we'd seen Jamie off to hospital, Cody and I joined Steele in the back of the limo for the short ride into town.

Rosie was waiting on the steps of the pub. She rushed over as soon as Cody got out of the car.

"That's one boy who's going to be in a lot of trouble," Steele murmured.

"You think so? You don't know much about mothers."

Rosie swept him into her arms and sobbed into his wet hair. I grinned. Maybe tomorrow there'd be consequences, but tonight she was so relieved to have him back that she was all but crushing the life out of him. He took it pretty well. Maybe he was happy to see her, too, after a scare like that.

"Well, I'll see you later," I said to Rosie. Across the road, a familiar black cat sat in my kitchen window, gazing down on the street.

"Don't go," she said, releasing her death grip on Cody long enough to smile at me. "Come inside and let me buy you a drink. Both of you. Everyone's inside celebrating."

I indicated my muddy jeans. "I'm a bit of a mess."

"So go home and change. It's not exactly a long way, is it?"

She waited expectantly until I agreed. I crossed the street—great, now the shaper even knew where I lived—and took the stairs two at a time. Might as well hurry up and get this over with. At least he couldn't threaten me with his fire while there were other people around.

I see you found them, Syl said as I came in. **Where's Jamie?**

"He's gone to hospital. Broken leg."

I filled her in as I changed out of my wet clothes. I would have preferred a bath and an early night, but Rosie was waiting.

Unfortunately, so was Jake Steele.

"He has scars all over his back," I told Syl.

Who, Jamie?

"No. Jake Steele."

She blinked. **That was quick work. You've known the man a couple of hours, and you've already had his clothes off?**

"Ha ha. He took his shirt off to splint Jamie's leg."

She flicked her tail angrily, changing moods like the wind. **You shouldn't be hanging around with him. Or feeling sorry for his poor scarred back. The man's a shaper.**

"I know, I know. Believe me, it wasn't my choice."

If it wasn't for shapers, we wouldn't be here in Berkley's Bay, hiding from the world. If it wasn't for shapers, a certain apartment block in Crosston would still be standing, its residents' lives untouched by fire, and Syl herself wouldn't be hiding in her cat form, too scared to face the world as a human again.

And if it wasn't for shapers, I wouldn't have been driven out of my home in the first place.

Shapers were bad news, full stop. No matter how good they looked with their shirts off.

"Do you want to come with me?"

She gave me a look of disdain. **Are you kidding me? I'm not spending any more time with that guy than I have to. I don't want him outing me.**

"No one else in town has guessed you're a shifter—not even the other shifters."

No one else in town is a fireshaper. She turned her back on me and started grooming herself. Conversation over.

"I'll see you later, then." She was probably right to avoid him. I should have done the same.

I crossed the street, avoiding the puddles. The sky was clearing now; a few stars had poked their heads out from behind the clouds. I hesitated on the threshold of the pub, wishing I'd been faster to come up with an excuse for Rosie. I really didn't want to spend any more time with Jake Steele. I'd caught him watching me a few times tonight, and the hostility in his eyes made me uneasy. I couldn't think what I'd done to deserve it, but nothing good ever came of catching a shaper's attention. They didn't need a reason for the things they did. They were like a force of nature. Might as well stand in the path of a forest fire and tell it to stop burning.

Noise and light burst on me as I opened the inner door and stepped inside.

"Here's my hero!" Rosie cried when she caught sight of me standing in the doorway. Heads turned, and several people cheered. I felt my cheeks heating, and hurried to join her at the bar. Having so many people staring at me at once made me uneasy, especially since one of them was Jake Steele. He was seated at a table with Joe's parents, who were the alphas of the local werewolf pack. Joe's mum Norma waved to me and I nodded, but I wasn't going over there to say hello. I'd had quite enough of Mr Steele for one evening.

Rosie threw a grateful arm around me and dragged me back to the bar. Cody was propped on a stool with a nearly empty glass of lemonade in front of him. Joe and Holly sat beside him, and Joe enveloped me in a hug that would have done a bear proud.

Embarrassed by the attention, I looked everywhere but at them, and found my eye drawn to the sign prominently displayed above the bar. “No Shifting on the Premises, by Order of the Publican,” it read, in large black letters. Some comedian had gotten up on the bar one night and drawn a set of fangs in the corner, with a single drop of blood rolling off them. Alberto had never bothered to remove the graffiti. Perhaps he secretly approved of the threat.

I’d certainly never seen anyone shift in here, except for Joe tonight, and he’d been shifting from animal to human. I had the feeling Alberto’s objection was to going the other way, from human to animal. Bar fights got bad enough when everyone stayed human, without throwing fangs and claws into the mix.

Not that there were many bar fights in here. When the owner was a vampire, people tended to be on their best behaviour. Alberto was a local legend—I’d heard some crazy stories about him since arriving in Berkley’s Bay. One guy swore he’d seen the ground open up and swallow him one night, others said they’d heard raised voices from behind the locked door to the cellar, though no one but Alberto was ever seen to come and go through that door. This had led to a favourite theory among those who resented the vampire’s status in town: that he kept prisoners down there to use as blood donors. Even Joe, who was usually pretty level-headed, insisted that he’d seen Alberto in broad daylight once, walking in the wilderness beyond the town.

"Thank you for finding him," Holly said, giving me a slightly less excitable but no less sincere hug of her own.

"What'll you have?" Joe asked. "I'm going to buy you a drink."

"You really don't have to do that," I began, but he cut me off with a wave of his big hand, so I let him order a rum and Coke. Just one drink, to make him happy.

"How did you manage to find him?" Rosie asked. She had one arm around her son, and now she ruffled his hair. "The little devil was well and truly off the beaten track, he tells me."

"Mum!" He pushed her hand away, but he was smiling.

They all looked at me expectantly.

"There was too much rain out there to pick up a trail," Joe said.

"If you have some secret way of tracking down missing children, I want to know." Holly rubbed her hugely pregnant stomach meaningfully. "It could come in handy one day soon."

"Just got lucky." I took a swig of rum and Coke, and felt the alcohol burn a warm trail all the way down my throat.

"Really?" Rosie looked doubtful. "The way Mr Steele told it, you left the track and went haring off like a bloodhound on a scent."

Damn the man. I glanced across and found him looking back at me. I lowered my eyes to the bubbles in my drink.

"How did you know where to start looking?" Rosie was persistent. "It was nowhere near where the boys left their bags."

"Just a hunch."

"Well, thank goodness for hunches, then." Rosie still didn't look convinced, but she gave me a quick, fierce hug. "Thanks again. I'd better take him home. Too much excitement for a school night."

Cody hugged his dad and Holly, then he and Rosie went over to say goodbye to his grandparents. Steele too, though he didn't get any hugs. Fireshapers just weren't the cuddly type. When they'd gone the fireshaper in question glanced my way again.

Holly nudged me. "He keeps looking at you. I think he fancies you."

"Oh, shush. That's the pregnancy hormones talking. You just want everyone to make babies."

She laughed. "I do not. I wouldn't wish this on my worst enemy. Sore back, swollen ankles, heartburn. I'm living on three hours' sleep a night and I have a stomach the size of an elephant. And shifting just makes it worse. It's torture."

"Never mind. Not long to go now." She was due in three more weeks. "Then Joe can help and you can get some more sleep."

"I'm helping now," Joe protested. "Who do you think rubs her feet, and her back, and brings her snacks when she can't be bothered getting out of her chair?"

She whacked his arm. "Can't be *bothered*? You try heaving twelve extra kilos around with you all day and see how easy it is to get up."

He grinned. "You don't know how I suffer, Lexi. All that back rubbing is damaging my delicate hands."

He held out his hands for my inspection. They were nearly the size of dinner plates. Joe was a big guy, solid as well as tall. It would be hard to imagine anything less delicate.

"You, suffer? Your wife spoils you rotten."

"It's all an act," he said solemnly. "You should see how she treats me when we're alone."

Holly rolled her eyes at me. She barely came up to his shoulder. Even pregnant, she probably still only weighed half what her husband did.

"I imagine she's terrifying," I said dryly.

We chatted for a while, and Joe bought me another drink, though I'd only meant to stay for one. They were both good company, though a little more subdued than normal. Holly's pretty face took on a grim look every time the Mayor's braying laugh rose above the noise in the pub, though she kept up such a flow of chatter that no one who didn't know her well would have realised there was anything wrong. It made me want to walk right over and punch him in his smug face. He'd kicked Holly out on the flimsiest pretext so he could give the job to his girlfriend's niece. That might come back to bite him in the arse when the kid screwed it up, and none of us would be upset.

They were my kind of people, Joe and Holly, and I hated to see them so down. Friends had been few enough in my life that I treasured every one I had. Even Syl liked them, prepared to overlook the fact that they were wolves. We'd shared a pizza and a bottle of wine on many a Friday night since we'd moved in. No wine for Holly, of course. I'd been forced to drink her share.

The noise in the pub had reached a dull roar and my glass was nearly empty again when Holly nodded behind me, a gleam of mischief in her eye. I turned to find Steele at my elbow.

"Hi, I'm Jacob Steele," he said, leaning across me to shake hands with Joe. A wave of heat came off his body as he brushed against me, and I moved back ever so slightly. "We didn't meet properly before."

"Joe Kincaid, and this is my wife, Holly. Thank you for your help in finding the boys."

"It wasn't me," he said, flashing a practised smile. "It was all Lexi's doing. Can I buy you all a drink?"

Holly smiled her dimpled smile at him, though there was a certain wariness there, too. They hadn't forgotten who he was: one of the most powerful shapers on the Ruby Council. Despite the number of humans around, this was shaper territory.

Shapers, just as much as anyone, liked the benefits that industrialisation and human ingenuity had brought to the world. The Great War had ended nearly a hundred years ago with a truce that guaranteed shaper access to human manufacturing, in return for more human-only territory and the right to share the shapers' lands. But the Ruby Council ruled this part of the country and, if their grip on the reins was generally light, it didn't do to forget that they could tighten that grip at any moment.

This man with his fake smiles governed the whole of the South-East, which basically made him Lord of All He Surveyed around here. Shapers tended to be a little arbitrary in their decisions, as Holly had so recently discovered, and there wasn't a damn thing anyone else could do about it.

I didn't trust that smile. The memory of his casual threats in the bookshop was still front and centre in my mind.

"Not for me, thanks," Holly said. "It's time this pregnant lady went home. I need sleep and a back rub, not necessarily in that order."

"I guess that's my cue to leave too," Joe said, flexing his hands melodramatically. "She's going to work these fingers to stumps."

I snorted. "You'll live."

I should have gone with them. I meant to, but when I turned back to say goodbye to Alberto, he'd placed another full glass in front of me, ice clinking invitingly.

Steele patted my stool. "Sit down. Just one more. We haven't had a chance to chat yet."

Exactly. And that was just the way I liked it. "I'm not sure I like your brand of small talk, Mr Steele."

I raised the glass to my lips and downed half of it in one go. This could be the shortest chat on record. Alberto wiped his precious bar top, though it was already sparkling clean. Maybe he'd be interested in hearing about the threat to his beloved bookshop if Steele got too insistent.

"You're different," he said. "Nothing personal, but different usually means trouble. It's my job to deal with trouble."

He thought being different caused trouble? He should try walking a mile in my shoes.

"It seems to work out all right for you shapers."

His eyes narrowed. "Things would go much easier for you if you answered the question."

So we were back to threats again. My heartrate picked up the pace. At least there were witnesses here. Alberto was engrossed in conversation with the guy on the fireshaper's other side. Steele wouldn't try anything in front of all these people, would he? "You haven't asked one yet. But there's nothing special about me. I'm one hundred per cent regular old human."

He leaned closer, his blue eyes frosty. "I'd really like to believe you. But I don't."

"Is there a problem here?" Alberto's smooth tones cut across the menace in the air.

Steele sat back and took a sip of his drink. "Not at all. Just having a friendly chat."

Friendly, my arse.

Alberto wasn't convinced either. "Good." Steele wasn't the only one who could plaster on a fake smile. "Because Lexi is a personal friend of mine. She's an asset to our town. The bookshop never ran so smoothly before she arrived."

I smiled gratefully at him. No one did veiled threats like a vampire.

"I'm glad to hear it." Not that Steele looked particularly cowed. Even a vampire would have to get lucky to bring down a shaper of his power. "Sometimes the enemy who hides in plain sight is deadlier than those who lurk in the shadows."

"No shadows here," Alberto said, with an emphatic shake of his head. "Lexi is one hundred per cent pure sunshine."

I looked from one to the other, confused. Enemies and shadows? It sounded like a whole other conversation was going on under the surface here. After a moment, Steele nodded, and the smile he cast my way was the friendliest expression I'd seen on his face yet.

"What brings you to Berkley's Bay?" Alberto asked, swiping at non-existent spots on the bar's gleaming surface. "Something particular, or just a yearning for the sea air?"

"Various things. I'll need to talk to you when it's convenient," Steele said noncommittally. "I wish I had time for sea air, but the Mayor's been bending my ear half the night, so it sounds like I'll be busy."

Oops. I looked down at my glass. Hope one of those ear-bending things wasn't his missing altarpiece.

"I'm surprised the Ruby Adept could spare you. I hear you're the rising star of the council."

"No, that's Anders," he said, a certain bitterness in his voice. I jumped at the mention of that hated name, but neither of them noticed. "I'm far from being the Ruby Adept's favourite person at the moment. In fact, I could be here quite a while. He basically told me not to hurry back."

Oh, joy. Nothing ever happened in sleepy Berkley's Bay, which was why Syl and I had chosen it. We needed a place to lay low, far from the city, somewhere no one would think to look for us. Having a councillor in residence—and one who was already suspicious of me—really didn't fit in with my plans.

The last councillor I'd known had involved himself in robbery, blackmail, and murder. I took another swig of my drink, feeling the burn all the way down my throat. I shivered anyway. At least it didn't sound like Steele was on good terms with Anders.

No sooner had I put down the empty glass than Alberto replaced it with another. Apparently satisfied I was in no immediate danger from the councillor, he went to serve someone else.

Steele's own drink sat before him, still half full. Scotch on ice, judging by its honey gold colour.

"Let's start again," he said, taking a sip. His pale blue eyes watched me over the rim of the glass. Very striking. "Alberto vouches for you, so perhaps I was hasty. Tell me about yourself."

"There's nothing to tell," I said, wary in spite of all the alcohol I'd consumed. He should have stuck to threats. There was no way he was charming the information he wanted out of me.

"You're new here, aren't you? I don't remember seeing you last time I was out this way. And I *would* remember."

"Are you flirting with me?"

He laughed. "Are you always this direct?"

I downed the glass and gave him a fake smile of my own. Did he really think he could flutter his eyelashes and win me over?

"I'm going home."

I wouldn't trust him any farther than I could throw

him—and, considering the well-muscled height of him, that wouldn't be far. He was way too nosy for my taste. Although, in other ways, he was *exactly* to my taste. My gaze lingered on the broad shoulders, then travelled down a muscled arm to the strong hand holding his glass. What would those hands feel like on my skin? Pity about his personality. In other circumstances I would have enjoyed finding out.

"So soon?"

"It's been a busy evening, and I've got work in the morning."

"That's a shame. Let me walk you home."

"Seriously? It's just across the street." I hopped off the stool, but somehow fumbled the landing, my head whirling from the unaccustomed alcohol. I staggered and fell against him. For a moment my face was solidly planted against his muscular chest.

His hands closed on my shoulders and gently set me on my feet again. Not quite what I'd imagined when I'd been picturing his hands on my body. My cheeks flamed.

"Maybe I'll just come and make sure you get there in one piece." There was laughter in his voice.

"I'm fine, really." I clung to what was left of my dignity. "I think I got my foot caught on something."

He ignored me, steering me toward the door with one hand in the small of my back. The heat of it burned through my shirt. Well, it was only across the street. I gritted my teeth and kept moving.

The night air felt good on my heated skin. Refreshing. My head cleared a little as I marched across the street, determined to put some distance between us. I fumbled the key in the lock on the street door, but I got it open in the end.

"Thanks for the drink."

His blue eyes glinted in the light from the streetlamps. "Maybe we can do it again some time."

Over my dead body. "I'm sure you'll be too busy with your councillor duties."

He refused to take the hint. "I don't work twenty-four seven. All rest and no play, as they say …"

"Goodnight." I stepped inside and shut the door firmly. He'd just have to find someone else to play with.

5

I had piles of books all over the counter when Joe's mum Norma came in. She was in her fifties, though she didn't look much more than forty. One of the benefits of the shifter life: they didn't show their age like humans did. Maybe that was why so many humans wanted to be turned. Shifters were always popular among the humans in shaper towns.

Of course, it was a different story in the human territories. A shifter would be risking their life to travel there, which was why Syl and I had been forced to hide out in shaper territory.

Norma wore a sleeveless sundress which made me shiver just looking at it; I had a long-sleeved shirt on and I'd been looking around for my sweater. Werewolf metabolisms ran hotter than other people's—apart from fireshapers, of course. Steele, for example, had been warm to the touch last night.

Though why I should be thinking about touching *him* I didn't know. Impatiently, I pushed him out of my mind and smiled at Norma instead.

"You look nice. Have you just had your hair done?" Tegan's salon was next door. We had a lot of customers in common.

She patted her softly waved hair self-consciously. "Yes. I thought I'd better make an effort for the baby shower tomorrow. You're still coming, aren't you?"

"Of course. Wouldn't miss it for the world."

Liar, said Syl. **A whole lot of women playing silly games with nappies and telling horror stories about the birth of their children? Who in their right mind would want to go to that?**

She was perched on a pile of books in the window display, her pink tongue flicking in and out as she groomed herself.

Babies are pretty cute. Cuter than some cats I know. And I couldn't help being caught up in Joe and Holly's excitement for their first child together. Cody was hoping for a little brother, but I had a suspicion that Norma had her heart set on a little granddaughter. Either way, there were a lot of people looking forward to this new little person's arrival.

"Do you think you could pick up the cake from the bakery for me? I was going to duck in and get it in the morning but I'm not sure I'll have time. All that excitement last night cut into my preparations a bit."

"What excitement?" My mind was still preoccupied with the problem of Jake Steele and his odd questions, so I was a little slow.

She laughed. "What excitement, she says. Only finding my lost grandson and his friend. You're something of a celebrity now, you know, you and your mysterious talents."

"Really, it wasn't a big deal. It could have been anyone who found them."

"Well, it's all the girls next door are talking about this morning."

Great, said Syl, favouring me with a death stare. Cats did that so well.

Don't give me that look. What was I supposed to do, leave them out there all night?

When Norma left, I went back to sorting the piles. One of my regulars had brought in two huge boxes of books; I hadn't taken everything he had, but I still had plenty to price and find a home for on the shelves.

There was the usual collection of shifter and shaper romances. Shaper romances seemed particularly popular among the residents of Berkley's Bay. They usually featured some poor human girl swept off her feet by a dashing shaper—or dazzled by his wealth, more like.

A children's book of myths and legends at the bottom of the box caught my eye as I lifted it out. I flicked through, admiring the watercolour illustrations. There was a lovely one of Hades, done in moody blues and purples. His chariot was erupting out of the ground, surrounded by swirls of darkness, clods of earth flying from under his horses' hooves as he leaned over, about to snatch up the shrinking Persephone. The contrast between his dark domain and Persephone's sunlit world was stark. No wonder the pretty nature goddess hated living in the gloomy underworld.

I turned a few more pages and found another gorgeous picture, this one of Prometheus, chained to his rock while the eagle snacked on his liver as punishment for bringing fire to mankind and creating the first fireshapers. In the clouds above, Hephaistos, blacksmith to the gods, and the one who'd sneaked the fire to Prometheus, pleaded on his knees for mercy, while Zeus gazed into the distance with a look that said *No way, José.*

The next legend dealt with Zeus's jealousy, and his creation of the airshapers so that he, too, would have a special group of followers, but I snapped the book shut. Stupid children's stories. Even in the quiet haven of my bookshop I had to have shapers rammed in my face.

Once the morning sun left the front window, Syl retired to her cushion on the counter. She was unusually quiet this morning. Guess that made two of us. I sorted like a demon and tried to ignore the uneasiness growing inside me.

Just before lunch, the main source of my uneasiness entered the shop, setting the bell to jangling wildly. Why couldn't he just do whatever it was he'd come to do, and get his undeniably cute shaper arse back to the city? He'd better not try his flaming threats again.

"Hi." He took off his sunglasses and offered one of his dazzling smiles. Looked like he was still trying to win me over with his charm. He was gorgeous when he smiled, and I felt a moment's genuine regret that I couldn't smile right back. When was the last time anyone had looked at me like that? "How about I buy you lunch?"

"How about no thanks?" My moment's regret soon passed—it didn't matter how pretty he was, he was still a shaper.

"Why not? You have something else booked?"

"No. I'm just busy."

"Really?" He set his sunglasses down on the counter and looked around in a very theatrical way, like a pantomime star searching for the villain. "You don't seem to be overrun with customers."

"Really."

He stroked Syl and she got up and stalked away down the counter.

I hid a smile. "I have books to sort and new stock to price. Things to do."

To demonstrate just how busy I was, I swept an armful of detective novels off the counter and went over to the crime shelves to make room for them.

"You still have to eat."

Clearly Councillor Steele wasn't used to having people turn him down. I cast him an impatient glance over my shoulder. He had one hip propped against the counter, muscular arms folded across his broad chest. My gaze lingered for a moment. If he hadn't been a shaper—but he was, so there was no point thinking about it.

Besides, I liked my men a lot less bossy. And less flammable.

"Sorry. Too busy."

"Shame. It would do my reputation good to be seen out with you. You're quite the celebrity in town today."

Why is he still here? Syl complained, winding around my ankles as I shelved the last book.

Because he's a giant pain in the butt. Would you stop that? You're getting fur all over my jeans. I said nothing to Steele. I was beginning to think just ignoring him might be the best strategy.

"Everyone's talking about you, you know."

"Well, people talk." I went back behind the counter; I felt better with a barrier between us. "There's not much else to do in a little town like this. The most exciting thing that happens here is the occasional visit from the Councillor."

Those pale blue eyes of his lit with amusement. "So you find me exciting?"

Idiot. Syl leapt up onto the counter and rubbed her

head against my hip. More cat fur. **You walked right into that one.**

"I find you an interruption. If there's nothing I can help you with, I have a lot to do."

Couldn't say it much plainer than that, but he refused to take the hint.

"Some of the humans are wondering if you're a shifter."

Ridiculous. Syl licked her privates to show what she thought of that idea.

I returned his challenging gaze with a calm one of my own. "They should know by now that I'm not."

"Well, the shifters know that, of course," he said, "but that doesn't stop the rumours from spreading."

I shrugged. "I can't stop people believing what they want to believe."

"True." He leaned forward, lowering his voice. "Some people will believe anything. According to some people, those One Worlders have found a new weapon against shapers."

My heart began to beat a little faster. A smile still played around his lips, but those pale blue eyes watched me like a hawk, waiting to see my reaction. Now we were getting to his real reason for inviting me out to lunch. All his flirting was just a cover.

I forced myself to smile back and pretend a nonchalance I didn't feel. "Really? How'd they do that?"

I had no love for One Worlders, though I shared their dislike of shapers. The movement had been around since the end of the Great War, but it had gained traction in the last few years. It seemed the more time passed since the war, the worse people's memories got. As if, in this modern age of electricity and long-distance communication, people couldn't quite believe that the shapers had really destroyed all those cities, burying them beneath mountains or drowning them in the sea. Killed all those people with a flick of their fingers. And hey, there were more humans all the time, and so few shapers, that if humanity tried again, they really ought to be able to win the whole world for themselves—especially now that we had modern weapons on our side. Bullets killed shapers as easily as they did regular humans.

I knew it didn't work like that. Shapers didn't need to be numerous to be powerful, and their power no longer rested solely on what they could do, but on their wealth and influence. And besides, the One Worlders wanted to rid the world of shifters as well, and that didn't sit well with me. I liked the shifters I knew a darn sight better than I liked most humans.

"I thought you might tell me."

You could have heard a pin drop in the shop. The counter between us was no protection at all. The suspicion was back in his eyes, and it was broad daylight. No chance of Alberto rescuing me now.

"I have no idea."

"And yet you went straight to those boys as if they were a homing beacon. Normal people can't do that. So prove to me that you're normal and tell me how you did it."

"I don't believe in that One World shit. Some of my best friends are shifters." He watched me, saying nothing, and my heart began to pound. I thought I'd left this garbage behind in Newport. Everyone suspicious of everybody else—couldn't we just agree the world was big enough to share and leave it at that? "Do you think I'd be living here, in the middle of shaper territory, if I belonged to the One World cult?"

He folded his arms. "You've never heard of people infiltrating a society to work against it from within?"

Those enemies hidden in plain sight that he'd mentioned to Alberto in the pub last night. He'd seemed to give up his suspicions when Alberto had vouched for me, but he must have been thinking it over, and he couldn't let go of how I'd led him straight to the lost boys.

"Sure I've heard of that." Couldn't he just leave me alone? "And if I was doing that, I would have pushed you down a dark hole in the bush last night, *with pleasure*."

Holy shit, will you watch your mouth? Syl gasped in my head.

But Steele threw back his head and laughed, and the tension in the room dissipated as if it had never been. Well, fancy that—a shaper with a sense of humour. Colour me amazed.

Syl looked from him to me then back again, her tail twitching in agitation. One paw darted out and knocked his sunglasses off the counter.

He bent to pick them up, still smiling. "I don't think your cat likes me."

"My cat has excellent taste."

He fiddled with the glasses a moment, then put them back on. "Are you sure I can't persuade you to come to lunch with me?"

He knows you're hiding something, Syl said, glaring at him through slitted eyes.

"Positive."

He left, and I breathed a sigh of relief as the door jangled shut behind him.

"Of course he knows." My shoulders slumped and I leaned heavily on the counter. "But he can't prove anything. Dammit!"

I pounded the counter in frustration. Syl leap into the air, then sat down and tried to pretend I hadn't startled her.

"Why did he have to come here?"

Syl rubbed her head against my cheek. Absently I stroked her, trying to think what to do. Maybe he'd finish his business here, and go; then I wouldn't have to do anything. But if he kept sniffing around …

Should we leave? Syl's green eyes were serious. She watched me, unblinking.

"I don't *want* to leave. I like it here. We have friends—Alberto has been wonderful, and Holly's baby is due soon."

I didn't want to slip out of here in the night and never see these people again. But I couldn't afford this kind of attention, either—especially not from a shaper.

Not when our safety depended on anonymity. Not when Anders could still be looking for us.

A horrible thought struck me. "Do you think he's working with Anders?"

Lord, why hadn't I thought of that before? Steele had seemed suspicious of me right from the start. Following me around, telling me I wasn't a sheep. And Anders was on the council, too. But it hadn't sounded like they got on, when Steele had mentioned him in the pub last night.

And if he'd come to take me away, what was stopping him? He'd said he had business with Alberto. Suddenly it seemed imperative to find out exactly what that business was.

Syl's ears flattened against her head. **We should leave. We can't take the risk.**

Though my heart was pounding, I found myself arguing. "But we don't know for sure."

I thought of Holly, and of the nursery, all fitted out in readiness for its new occupant. I'd been looking forward to meeting that new little person. And Holly would need help, with Joe busy trying to make up for her lost wages. It would be a shame to run out on her for nothing.

And yet—visions of a burning building came to me. The reek of smoke invaded my nostrils. We still didn't know if all our former neighbours had managed to escape the firestorm Anders had unleashed on them because of me. If I stayed, would I be putting Holly in danger?

"We don't know enough to make a decision. We need to find out why he's really here first."

Syl's tail lashed in agitation. *_How do you propose doing that? You going to ask him if he's hunting a werecat and a girl with a peculiar gift?_*

"I could head out to his place tonight and snoop around, see what I can find out."

And by snoop around_, you mean use your gifts to spy on him? That sounds like an excellent plan, when he's already suspicious of you, and for all we know may have a way of detecting your powers in action._

"Right." She had a point there. Maybe not the best idea to flaunt my abilities right under his nose. "I guess I could talk to Alberto, see if he'll tell me what Steele is doing here."

Tonight?

Alberto usually didn't rise until around six o'clock in the evening. If he didn't come over to the shop tonight, I'd head over to the pub to meet him as soon as I'd closed up.

"Yes. Tonight."

6

But Alberto wasn't at the pub that night. The barman said he was dining with Jake Steele. Figured. Even when he wasn't there, Steele was a pain in my arse. I'd have to try to catch Alberto early on Saturday evening, before things got too hectic at the pub.

If I survived the baby shower, at least. I arrived at Norma and Ray's house at two o'clock on Saturday afternoon, having shut the shop a little early, wearing my one and only skirt. I figured if Norma had got her hair done, I needed to make a bit more effort than my usual jeans and T-shirt.

They lived in a small brick bungalow on a large block of land that backed onto the bush, perfect for escaping on full moon nights. Holly met me at the door, perfectly at home in her mother-in-law's house.

"You look nice," she said. "Did you bring a baby photo of yourself?"

Crap. The invitation had mentioned it, but I'd shoved that into a drawer and forgotten all about it.

"No. Sorry! I don't have any."

"Didn't you ask your mum?"

It was only then, staring at this person that I saw every day, this person I considered a friend, that I realised how cautious I'd become. Holly didn't know the first thing about me, despite all the pizzas we'd shared.

"My mother and I … don't talk anymore."

"Oh, I'm sorry. I didn't realise."

"It's fine." It really wasn't, but this was hardly the time for such a conversation. "Is everyone else here?"

"Nearly. Come and let me introduce you."

I already knew most of the women: some of Holly's now-former workmates, a couple of girls she'd grown up with who still lived locally. I met Norma's next-door neighbour, a rather round lady who was already eyeing the cupcakes, and then Tegan burst in, in her usual scene-stealing style.

"Sorry I'm late! You should have started without me." She took a glass of champagne and plonked her ample backside into the chair next to me. "I hate baby showers," she muttered. "No one enjoys them except the expectant mum. Still, I suppose she needs something to perk her up before her life is totally destroyed, eh?"

She handed over her own baby photo and Holly laughed.

"Tegan, what's the point of putting this up on the wall? It's supposed to be a competition, to see if everyone can guess which baby photo goes with which guest." She waved the offending photo, and everyone laughed. It showed a tiger cub.

Tegan shrugged. "It was the only one I had."

Typical Tegan. I sipped my own champagne and smiled. There was a good mix of shifters and humans here. Holly and Norma were wolves, of course. Tegan was a tiger, and a couple of the others were bears. It was pretty common to see shifters and non-shifters socialising in the shaper-controlled cities. Some of the humans who moved into shaper territory were groupies, hoping to find some accommodating shifter to turn them. Even Alberto had his suitors; despite the drawbacks, there were still plenty of people wishing to become vampires.

Others were drawn by the generally better living conditions in shaper territory. The laws might be draconian, and justice swift—but, unless you were a criminal, that generally didn't affect you. Room to breathe was a lot more appealing to many people than being crammed in cheek-by-jowl in the overcrowded human-controlled cities. There was a reason the One Worlders were eyeing the amount of land under shaper control and agitating for a forcible redistribution.

And there were always a few who plain old hated

shifters, hated shapers ... hated anything that smacked of magic or "the devil". Yet they still made their homes in shaper territory—sometimes out of a misguided wish to "minister" to the poor deluded humans who actually liked living there, but sometimes just because they were hypocritical enough to prefer the living conditions there, whatever they thought of the neighbours. Some were better at disguising their dislike than others. You've never seen two-faced until you've seen a One Worlder trying to live unnoticed in a shaper town.

I had the feeling that Holly's friend Becky might be one of this type. She was a pretty blonde, with one of those round, butter-wouldn't-melt kind of faces. But every now and then I caught a slight curl to her full lips when she thought no one could see, particularly when she was looking at Holly's enormous belly, as if the very idea of another werewolf coming into the world revolted her.

I'd seen a few like her in Crosston. A big city like that attracted all sorts of people. As long as they didn't do anything with their loathing, the shapers generally left them in peace.

But Becky just seemed a little too bubbly, as if she were compensating for something. She clapped her hands together now. "Let's have some games!"

Norma obligingly organised a game that involved pegging baby clothes on a line one-handed. I got out early on, which suited me just fine. I was beginning to think Syl had been right about baby showers. I'd offered to bring her along, and she'd just laughed at me.

One of the many benefits of living as a cat is you don't have to put up with any of that bullshit, she'd said, flouncing ahead of me down the stairs to the street. *_I have other plans._*

Still, I liked Holly, and this was about her, not me, so I smiled and tried to look interested as tiny baby suits and little booties fell to the floor, owing to some very dodgy one-handed pegging. Those clothes were so small. It was hard to believe anyone could be so tiny.

As if summoned by thinking about her, Syl spoke in my head.

Have you started snoring yet?

It's not that bad, I lied. *_Where are you? What are you doing?_*

Our link didn't stretch too far. Since Syl wasn't actually an animal, linking with her wasn't the same as what I'd done in the bush the other night. I could feel animals from a long way away and enter their minds, even direct them to do things for me or see what they were seeing. With Syl, it was more like a radio communication. I could hear what she wanted me to hear, and she could hear whatever I chose to share, but the rest of her mind was just static, and the further apart we were, the worse the signal got until it dissolved into nothing. For me to hear Syl so clearly, she must be pretty close by. Since she hadn't been interested in the baby shower, I couldn't see any other reason for her to be so far from our apartment.

**Just exploring,* she said, with a nonchalance that didn't fool me for a second.

Exploring what? We've lived here for three months. What's to explore?

The clothes-hanging game ended with a round of applause, and one of the bear shifters was presented with her prize. The next game apparently involved a race to see who could drink the contents of a baby bottle the fastest, as a whole bunch of bottles were being filled and passed around. Tegan insisted on hers being filled with champagne.

**Just paying our friend a visit,* Syl said airily.

Distracted by the bottle of juice I'd been handed, I wasn't thinking. **Alberto?**

That didn't make sense, but our roster of friends was pretty small. Everyone knew Alberto spent the day sleeping in the extensive cellars he'd had built beneath the pub, though no one had actually seen them. Alberto discouraged visitors with a heavy iron door which he locked behind him once he'd retired for the morning. None of the staff even had access to the rooms beyond that door.

But if Syl was at the pub I wouldn't have been able to hear her. My brain finally caught up with that fact.

No, wait—you mean Steele? I thought we agreed it would be too dangerous to spy on him?

Her mental voice sounded impatient. **No, we agreed that* you *couldn't spy on him. We never said anything about* me.*

Holly shouted "Ready, set, go!" and everyone raised their baby bottles to their lips. I got a mouthful of super-sweet juice and pulled a face. Maybe I should have gone for the champagne, like Tegan.

Some of the ladies were taking the challenge seriously, sucking for all they were worth. I made a less enthusiastic attempt, distracted by my conversation with Syl. On the one hand, we needed to find out whatever we could about Steele and his reasons for being here, but on the other, one black cat was no match for a shaper. No matter how opinionated that cat was.

Is he home? I asked.

Doesn't seem to be.

Well, that was a relief, at least.

Big place, she said. **The guy must be loaded.**

Of course he's loaded. He's on the bloody Ruby Council. The fireshapers ruled half the country, and the Ruby Council ruled the fireshapers. **He could probably buy and sell this whole town and everyone in it out of petty cash.**

There's someone in the kitchen, she said a few moments later. **Looks like that caretaker woman who lives here. Can't* *see anyone else. No car in the driveway. If I can find an open window I'll go in and have a snoop around.**

Be careful.

Stop fussing. Go put a nappy on a baby doll or something.

Surreptitiously, I checked my watch. How much longer was I stuck here for?

I'd rather have been with Syl, that was for sure. Steele's property on the headland was a few streets away from Norma and Ray's place. Maybe I should head over there when the shower finished. Still, it was easier to explain away a trespassing cat than a human, and if Steele returned, or his housekeeper saw me, the explanations could get embarrassing. Maybe I could pretend I'd dropped something there the other night. An earring, perhaps?

Syl said nothing for a while. Holly brought out garbage bags with holes cut in them and solemnly instructed everyone to put them on and get into pairs. Tegan rolled her eyes as she struggled into hers. Just as well the bags were big.

"Who would like to volunteer to go first?" Holly asked.

Becky's hand shot into the air. "What are you going to do to us?"

Holly laughed. "You know how feeding babies can get messy sometimes? We're going to practise feeding each other baby food."

"That doesn't sound so hard," Becky's partner said, eyeing the garbage bag she wore doubtfully.

"I'm sure you'll do a wonderful job," Holly said, handing each of them an open jar of baby food and a spoon.

They waited, spoons poised above their jars.

"You have to feed each other at the same time." Holly grinned mischievously. "There's just one catch."

"There's always a catch," Tegan muttered darkly.

Holly produced two blindfolds from behind her back and everyone groaned. "You have to wear these while you're doing it."

Hey, nice bedroom, Syl said. Though she spoke into my mind, it was hard to hear her over the gales of laughter as Holly solemnly blindfolded each woman.

Where are you? Whose bedroom?

His, I assume. Man, it's the size of our whole apartment. You should see his bed!

I really didn't need to hear about Jake Steele's bed. *_Focus, Syl._*

_I_ am _focusing. It's enormous, and it's on this kind of pedestal thing, like he's the king of the world or something. Hey, I wonder if it vibrates?_

I think you're focusing on the wrong things, Sylvie. Forget the bed, are you inside?

No, I'm on his windowsill. One _of his windowsills. He has a private balcony too. Do you think he takes his ladies there to admire the sunset before they retire to the vibrating bed of sexual transcendence?_

Can we please stop talking about him and sexual anything? Are there any open windows?

Syl sighed. **Sometimes I miss opposable thumbs.**

For a moment I considered telling her to shift and open the balcony door, but I knew she wouldn't listen. She'd developed such a terror of being caught in human form that I worried she'd spend the rest of her life as a cat.

Distracted, I watched Becky smear baby food all over her partner's face, and almost get a spoon in the eye in return. Everyone around me was laughing helplessly. Tegan leaned across.

"Are you all right? You don't seem yourself."

"I'm fine." It was hard to be two places at once. I tried to focus on the two contestants in front of me. Holly had a stopwatch out. Apparently we would all be timed, and the team who managed to finish their "meals" fastest would be the winner. But most of me was listening for Syl, wishing I was on that windowsill with her—or, better yet, inside the house. The sooner she got in there, the faster she could leave.

Hang on, she said. **I think there's a car coming this way.**

Steele's place was at the end of a long, tree-lined road that wound up through the bush to the clifftop. There were no other houses along that road, so if Syl could hear a car there wasn't anywhere else it could be going.

You should leave now, before anyone sees you.

Keep your fur on. No one's going to take any notice of a cat.

Is it him? Don't let him see you. He knows what you look like.

Relax, would you?

A burst of laughter caught my attention, so I made sure to laugh, too. Didn't want Tegan thinking there was something wrong. Becky and her partner had just finished and ripped off their blindfolds. Everyone was laughing at the look on Becky's face as she saw how much slop had ended up down the front of her garbage bag.

Hey, said Syl. *What's he doing here?*

Who?

She cried out in fear, a wordless mental shriek.

Syl! I leapt out of my chair. Everyone stared.

Tegan jumped up too. Despite her size, she could move fast. "Lexi? What's wrong?"

Syl! Syl! Are you hurt? What's wrong?

But there was no reply. Syl was gone.

7

"Lexi! Are you ill? What's the matter?" Tegan's urgency finally penetrated my consciousness, and I dragged my mind back from its scattered points.

Everyone was staring at me.

"I'm fine," I mumbled, pulling off my garbage bag. "Fine. Just remembered … something really urgent." I was half out of the room already, fear propelling me as I made my excuses. "So sorry! I've got to go."

Norma followed me out to the car. "Are you sure you don't need help?"

That was alphas for you, always trying to run everybody else's lives. She meant well, but there was nothing she could do for me.

"Sorry to run out like this." I started the engine, but she still stood there, frowning at me.

"You know, there's a rumour going around that you're an earthshaper," she said.

"What?" Talk about a blast from the past. I'd been run out of Newport when a very similar rumour started circulating. "Why?"

She shrugged. "People talk. You know how it is. There are quite a few theories about how you managed to find those boys. That's one of them."

"Damn." But this was a shaper town, in the heart of shaper territory. No one would spit on me in the street here, or smash my windows, for a rumour like that. No one would beat my brother to a pulp and drag his broken body away on my account.

I shuddered at the memory and threw the car into reverse.

Norma stepped back. "I'm just saying—try not to draw any more attention to yourself."

I looked at her—really looked at her this time—wondering what she was really saying. Did she suspect my secret? Was she trying to warn me not to draw *Steele's* attention? Damn the rumour mill. I didn't want anyone looking too closely at me. Particularly not Jake bloody Steele.

"Thanks, Norma. Sorry, but I've got to run." I shivered again, hoping those words didn't turn out to be prophetic.

"Take care of yourself."

She stood in the drive and watched me until I rounded the corner and was lost to view. I drove fast, the little car hurtling around the corners, but as I approached the last bend before the road straightened out and ran in a long line up to Steele's massive gates, I slowed.

What was I going to do there? I was no match for a shaper.

I pulled over and stared out the windscreen at the verdant bush. My mind coursed out through the green, passing through those gates as though they didn't exist, hunting, hunting. Tiny minds lurked everywhere: lizards sunning themselves on the rocks of Steele's extensive gardens, sparrows hopping over the long green swell of the lawn in search of food. Cockatoos screeched in the towering gums, and a pair of rainbow lorikeets darted madly through the trees, swooping and soaring. I should have done this straight away, but I'd been so panicked that my first thought had been to get here as fast as possible.

I found no cat mind, no animal life at all inside the house—not even a mouse within the walls. The place was sterile. Dammit, why couldn't the man have a pet? I called the birds to me instead, and sent them winging towards the windows.

Why couldn't I find Syl? My hands tightened on the steering wheel. Was she out of range? But I'd gotten here so quickly. In human form? That one was so unlikely it wasn't even worth considering. Which left me with much more unpalatable choices: She was unconscious. She was dead.

Split between half a dozen consciousnesses, I searched the estate, peeking in at the windows, watching for movement anywhere. Nothing. If only I'd linked to Syl's sight like this, and seen whatever she had seen just before she screamed. *What's* he *doing here?* Who? And what had he done to Syl? But I'd been trying to stay present at the baby shower, so no one would realise what a freak I was.

The housekeeper was still working in the large open-plan kitchen. If something terrible had just happened here, it certainly hadn't disturbed her. I sent the birds circling wider, higher. Through their eyes I saw my own car, idling at the side of the road, but nothing else moved.

Syl had said someone had pulled up in a car. *What's* he *doing here?* Where was the other car? Nothing was parked in the driveway now. Where had he gone?

I let the birds go, and shrank back into my own skin. What should I do now? I put the car into gear and made a U-turn. All the way home, I scanned the streets for a small black cat, or maybe even a lithe girl with her long black hair in a neat plait down her back, but I saw nothing.

At home, I unlocked the door with shaking hands.

"Syl?" I called, but no black cat came to wind itself around my legs.

I strode through the apartment, but there was no one there. It was getting dark. The kitchen window was partly open, as always, so that Syl could come and go. I looked across the road at the lights of the pub on the corner. Alberto would rise soon.

That animal scream of fear echoed in my head. I had to speak to Alberto right now. I had to know what Jake Steele was doing in town.

And then I had to track the bastard down and get Syl back.

I took off my pretty skirt, and changed into dark jeans and a black sweater. Tied my hair back in a ponytail so it was off my face. Once it was fully dark, I'd head back out to Steele's house and see if I could find any traces of Syl. Maybe it hadn't been him who'd hurt her, but it had happened at his house. That made him at least partly responsible, and confirmed all my bad opinions of shapers. Back in Crosston, folks I'd known said the only good shaper was a dead one—though they didn't say that too loud.

Down the stairs I went, and back out into the street. The lights outside the pub glowed a soft welcome. Nothing could be seen of the lights inside, since Alberto had altered the décor to get rid of windows and install the double entryway. No drinkers spilled out onto the footpath from open doors, like most other pubs I'd been to. But then, I'd never been to a pub owned by a vampire before.

It was something of a tourist attraction for the town, in fact. Berkley's Bay didn't have a lot to offer in the winter months, but in summer it came alive with holidaymakers fighting for a place in the sun. Lots of visitors came for a drink or a meal at the famous pub, hoping to get a glimpse of its owner.

They often went away a little let-down. Alberto carefully cultivated an urbane persona. In person, he was disappointingly, resolutely, ordinary. Sometimes I wondered if he was hiding from something, too. Most vampires liked to make more of a splash. Disappointed visitors had to be content with the wild stories that circulated about his power. For the price of a beer, plenty of locals would be happy to tell stories of how he'd lifted a truck off a woman pinned in the street outside the pub, or his ability to dissipate into smoke, or appear out of nowhere. These tales tended to get wilder as the number of beers consumed rose, so I was never sure how much, if any, to believe, but they kept the tourists happy.

Alberto wasn't behind the bar when I pushed my way through the inner door, and I sighed in frustration. I tried again to reach Syl, but I'd been trying almost constantly since I'd lost her, and this time was no more successful than the others. It was like niggling at a sore tooth with your tongue. It hurts, but you just can't stop doing it.

A group of guys clustered around the tables in front of the big screen TV, watching the end of a football game. Joe was among them.

"Party over already?" he asked.

"I left early," I said. "Have you seen Syl anywhere?"

He shook his head. "She'll show up when she's hungry."

That was the trouble when your "cat" refused to come out as an actual person. Nobody took her disappearance seriously.

"What about Jake Steele?"

Joe raised an eyebrow. "Don't tell me you've succumbed to our councillor's charms? Lucas will be devastated."

"Lucas barely knows I'm alive," I shot back, but without my usual humour. It was an old conversation between us. Joe had been trying to set me up with his younger brother, Lucas, almost from the moment he'd met me. "His great interest in me only exists in your head."

I left Joe to his football and ordered a mineral water from the day barman. Settled on a barstool, my hands flat on the cool surface of the bar, I let my mind expand, spreading out through the town, touching little glowing sparks of life. I left the lesser ones, the lizards and scurrying insects. There was a limit to how many minds I could inhabit at once without losing track of them all. I tickled the minds of any dogs and cats I found, sending them searching. Cats were better for this sort of thing, since they were usually freer to roam than dogs. I found birds, too; birds were better still. No one ever looked up, or thought anything of a bird perched in a nearby tree or hopping along a windowsill. They were practically invisible. But it was late in the day for the birds; they were all focused on finding shelter for the night, and hard to divert to my purposes. I stared blankly between my fingers at the surface of the bar, focusing on pushing farther and farther, taking hold of more minds than I'd ever handled before in my panicked need to find Syl.

My creatures scurried, prowled and flew, prying into corners, peeking through windows. They found black cats for me, and every time my heart would rise with hope, only to plunge back down when I realised it wasn't the *right* black cat. I looked into the faces of a dozen dark-haired young women, but none of them were the *right* woman. Lost in my exploration, I forgot where my body was.

I jumped when someone spoke right next to me. My hand jerked, spilling water onto the gleaming surface of the bar.

"Mind if I sit here?"

It was a guy about my own age, maybe a little older. I hadn't seen him before. His leather jacket said *city dweller*, as did the shine on his shoes. He was smiling, waiting expectantly by the stool next to me.

"It's a free country," I said, turning my shoulder slightly so I faced more towards the guys watching TV. There were plenty of empty stools; why did he have to sit right next to me? If he tried hitting on me, I'd go join Joe. I wasn't in the mood for dealing with guys who fancied their chances. Besides, I could hardly string two sentences together, I was so distracted by the search going on outside these walls.

He ordered a drink, then turned so his knees brushed against me. "Did you watch the game?"

He gestured at the TV, where blokes in tight shorts and football jerseys were hugging each other in a frenzy. Joe was cheering, so I guess his team had won.

"I'm not much of a fan." I glanced at my watch. Where was Alberto? My creatures hadn't found any sign of Steele yet, either. I watched the door that led down to the cellars.

"You're the one who found those kids the other night, right?"

I looked closer. Did I know this guy? Had he been in the pub that night? He didn't look familiar.

"Yeah, that was me."

"How'd you do that?"

"Just got lucky." If I had a dollar for every time I'd said that lately, I'd be ordering one of the pub's fine steak dinners tonight instead of eating reheated pizza.

"Really? That's not what I heard." He leaned closer, close enough for me to smell the spirits on his breath. "You can tell me. You're a shaper, right? Some kind of weird shifter, maybe? I bet you've got a nose like a bloodhound on you."

"Nope. Just lucky." I said it more firmly this time and started to slide off my stool.

His hand shot out and closed around my upper arm. "I think you should tell me."

I jerked my arm, but he only tightened his grip. I pinned him with a killing look, wishing I had one of my knives on me. Hadn't thought I'd need one for a baby shower. "I think you should let go."

"You know, you don't want to count on being lucky like that again. Finding someone you've lost, I mean."

My breath caught. Did he mean Syl? Who *was* this guy? I searched his face: tawny, animal-coloured eyes. Broad, flat nose. Shaggy blonde hair falling in his face. A shifter of some kind? He smirked at me, giving nothing away.

I glared at him. "If you have something to say, just say it."

"This guy bothering you?" Joe loomed at my shoulder, looking bigger and meaner than usual.

The guy let go, and I rubbed my arm, scowling at him. Had he taken Syl? I'd teach him to mess with my friends.

"Why don't you take a hike, buddy?" Joe continued. "I think you've had enough."

The guy slid off his stool, looking Joe up and down, the smirk replaced by a sneer. He was nowhere near Joe's size, but it didn't seem to faze him. He leaned forward and sniffed at Joe.

Yep. Definitely a shifter. But what kind? Most of them knew better than to take on a werewolf.

"Go back to your kennel, dog. Nobody cares what you think."

He pushed right into Joe's face. If he thought that would make Joe step back, he was wrong. Joe shoved, hard, and the guy staggered back a pace.

He snarled, his face rippling as he did. Oh, Lord. No wonder he wasn't afraid of Joe. The guy was a lion.

I nearly fell off my stool in my haste to get away. Joe snatched it up, bringing it around as the lion roared. What good was a barstool against a lion? But there was no point shifting. Joe's wolf wouldn't be any match for it either.

The lion gathered itself to spring, the powerful muscles in its hindquarters bunching, its tail twitching in anticipation. Joe backed up, never taking his eyes off the beast.

Then a dark blur flashed between them, knocking Joe out of the way. The barstool clattered to the floorboards and the lion went down in a flurry of tawny limbs. It gave a strangled yelp, and then the only sound in the room was the awful slurping sound of a vampire feeding.

Alberto crouched over the beast, his face buried in its massive neck. I shrank closer to Joe. I'd never seen Alberto feed before. It wasn't pretty. No one in the pub dared move or speak, afraid to draw the vampire's attention.

Before our eyes, the lion shrank back into the form of a man, sprawled on his back, one arm outstretched, fingers clutching at nothing. His heels drummed on the floor, then fell still. His fingers relaxed.

At last Alberto lifted his head. His mouth and chin were covered in blood, gleaming wetly in the light. The shifter's neck was a ruin, torn and shredded. Blood covered his clothes and leaked down onto the floor, forming a small but spreading pool beneath him.

The door swung open, admitting Jake Steele. He stopped short at the scene laid out before him, his gaze taking in the overturned barstools, the ring of silent onlookers, the vampire crouched over his victim on the floor. And all the blood.

"Zeus's balls! What's going on here?"

8

Flames sprang to life in Steele's clenched fists and shivered up and down his arms. The little tableau froze as everyone stared at the fire licking over his skin. Neither Joe nor I dared move a muscle. Alberto, unblinking, watched from his crouch over the body on the floor. Shadows stirred and flocked around him, sucking the light from the room.

Slowly he rose, wreathed in darkness, and faced the flaming shaper. Steele was the only light in the room, flaring bright as fingers of shadow reached hungrily for him. It was easy to forget what Alberto was, when he served you a drink or chatted about the latest town gossip. Now his face was lost in shadow, the genial bartender I knew gone. All of a sudden the wild tales that circulated about him seemed a lot more convincing. Those looming shadows were terrifying. My heart pumped harder, and I wondered if he could hear it. Never before had I been afraid of Alberto.

If Steele was intimidated by the vampire, he didn't show it. "Who's that? Why did you attack him?"

Alberto nudged the body with his foot contemptuously. "He's a shifter."

Behind me someone cleared their throat. I dragged my gaze from the confrontation as Mayor Johnson came forward, his massive belly preceding him. He'd been one of the crowd watching the football.

His chins wobbled a little as he cleared his throat again. The man's self-importance grated on me.

"I saw what happened. This gentleman turned into a lion, and Mr Alinari attacked him." He cast a resentful glance at Alberto. "Just as well it's off season. This kind of thing is very bad for business. Tourists don't like it."

That was another reason I didn't like him, if I'd even needed one after what he'd done to Holly: his open dislike of Alberto.

The swirling shadows dissipated as Alberto laughed. "Trust you, Johnson. Bad for tourism? So is starting brawls in the pub. He should have read the sign."

Steele's eyes flicked to the sign above the bar. "No shifting on the premises?"

"By order of the publican," Alberto finished, his usual urbane smile now firmly back in place, though the effect was rather spoiled by the blood staining his chin. "My pub, my rules."

"I see." Steele released his flames and I breathed a sigh of relief. Looked like there wasn't going to be a showdown today. Who would win a battle between a fireshaper and a vampire? Shapers were generally considered to be all-powerful, but today I'd seen a side of Alberto I hadn't known existed. How could anybody move that fast? And where had those swirls of darkness come from? I'd never heard that vampires could do that. Maybe the rumours were right, and he really was something special.

Steele moved closer, bending over to inspect the body on the floor. "Lion shifter. You don't see those too often. Who is he?"

Alberto shrugged. "No idea. Never seen him before."

Steele raised his voice, looking around at the silent crowd. "Anybody know this guy?"

Nobody did.

Steele quirked an eyebrow at Johnson, who was still hovering anxiously. "One of your tourists, perhaps? I doubt he'll be paying you a return visit."

"Is he dead?" Johnson asked.

He certainly looked it. He was very pale—which was hardly surprising, given that there seemed to be more blood outside his body than in it. His throat was a bloody ruin; I was trying not to look too closely at that. It turned my stomach.

Steele crouched by the body. "No. See that? That gash is starting to heal."

"I'll have him taken into custody, then," Johnson said.

"What for? The crime of being attacked by a vampire?" Steele looked up at Alberto. "Like to tell me what happened? Other than that he shifted? Why did he shift?"

"He was about to attack Joe here."

Steele's attention swung to Joe, who looked very uncomfortable to find himself in the spotlight. "Oh? What was the problem?"

"The guy was being an arsehole," Joe muttered.

"Not usually considered a crime, either." Steele rose to his full commanding height and looked at Joe stonily.

"He was being an arsehole to *me*," I said impatiently. *And I think he kidnapped my friend.* But that part I had to keep to myself. At least if the shifter wasn't dead I might be able to find out what he'd done with Syl. "Joe saw he was bothering me and came over to help. The guy didn't take too kindly to that, so he shifted. He could have killed us both."

"You're a wolf, aren't you?" Steele asked Joe.

Joe nodded.

I hoped Joe wouldn't cop any flak for this, though if anyone was going to get into trouble it should be Alberto. Shaper law was simple: don't do anything to piss off the shapers. Many things that would be considered crimes in the human territories were brushed aside here, as long as no shaper was hurt or inconvenienced. Their police force, the provosts, handled mundane crimes, but the bigger issues were dealt with by the shapers themselves, and their justice was swift and without appeal.

Shifters were normally given the leeway to police their own internal squabbles. Since this guy was a shifter himself, he'd probably have no recourse against Alberto. Or Joe.

But there was that famous shaper unpredictability to consider and, as the Master of the South-East, Steele was the ultimate authority here.

He turned his cool blue gaze on me. "What was he doing to you? Did he physically attack you?"

"No. He was just talking."

"Asking questions?"

"No." It was none of his damned business anyway, but it bothered me that Steele somehow guessed he'd been asking questions. I felt no compunction about lying. "Just trying to pick me up."

His eyes searched my face, as if he knew I was lying. Uneasily, I wondered if shapers had some way to tell. Then he picked up one of the barstools lying on the floor and snapped off its metal leg. I jumped at the sound and the unexpectedness of the action. *What the hell?*

Fire ignited in his hands again and danced along the piece of metal between them. I took an instinctive step back.

"I hope you're going to pay me for that," Alberto said coolly.

"You can put it on my tab."

The metal glowed red-hot, though Steele handled it as if it weren't superheated. He bent the metal bar into a pretzel shape. It bent as easily as if it were made of soft clay. A few molten drops splashed onto the wooden floor and sizzled. Alberto frowned.

"That, too," Steele said, then he crouched down by the unconscious lion shifter again and rolled him roughly onto his face. He jerked the guy's wrists together behind his back and fitted the pretzel shape over them, moulding it until it formed a perfect set of unlockable handcuffs. The cuffs didn't appear to harm the shifter's skin in any way—which, considering the metal still glowed a dull red, showed Steele's extraordinary control of his fireshaping. Or maybe that was his metalshaping. It all seemed connected. No wonder he'd made it onto the council so young.

He hoisted the unconscious shifter over his shoulder as he stood, heedless of the blood.

"No need to bother yourself," he said to the mayor, "I'll take him with me."

Johnson didn't ask what Steele was going to do with him—Steele clearly outranked him—but I sure wondered. Why was he, one of the most powerful shapers in the country, bothering with a lowly barroom brawl? Was he protecting the guy? He'd had a funny look on his face when he bent down to inspect him. I wasn't convinced that he didn't know who he was. Was the shifter working for him? Maybe they were both working for Anders.

My head spun as the horrible possibilities mounted. I folded my arms across my chest and eyed him with suspicion. Now I was even more anxious to check out his home. Would I find Syl there?

Without another word Steele walked out, leaving everybody gaping after him. Alberto was the first to move.

"Excuse me," he said. "I need a change of clothes."

He needed a shower, actually. There was even blood in his hair, which was stiff with it and standing up at odd angles. He looked quite unlike his usual debonair self.

"Are you okay?" Joe asked as Alberto disappeared through the door marked "Private".

"Fine. You?"

"Yeah, I'm good." He was still staring at the door into Alberto's private rooms. "Never seen Alberto in action before. Wait until I tell Holly."

I was about to suggest it might not be the best thing to describe to a pregnant woman, but then I gave a mental shrug. They were both werewolves. The look of admiration on his face told me he had a different view of such things than I did.

"Thanks for helping me out there," I said.

"No problem." He smiled at me. He had a kind face—not particularly good-looking, but kind. "I'll walk you home, make sure you don't run into any more trouble."

I rolled my eyes. "What kind of trouble am I going to get into crossing the street? No one's going to jump me between here and my front door."

"A pretty girl like you can't be too careful, you know." He frowned at me, mock-serious, as he held open the door. I knew he was just talking shit, to calm me after the bloody scene in the pub. He was a good guy. "What you need is a nice young man to look after you."

"Is that right?" He meant Lucas, of course, but I was barely listening. If Steele had Syl, things were going to get ugly. There was no way I could take on a shaper directly. "And I suppose you know just the person?"

"As a matter of fact, I do."

It was a cool evening, but at least it wasn't raining. A sprinkling of stars twinkled down on the bustling epicentre of Berkley's Bay. A few cars sat outside the pub, but we were the only people on the street. All the shops were dark. We crossed the road, our footsteps echoing on the pavement, me already planning the best way to get into Steele's house without being seen.

"Werewolves make great partners, you know," he continued. "Loving, committed—did you know they mate for life?"

"I believe you may have mentioned it a time or two." I watched in a fever of impatience as he fumbled his keys out of his pocket and unlocked the street door. Couldn't he go any faster? Pretending I had nothing more in mind than an evening in front of the TV was killing me. "But only if both parties are werewolves, so it doesn't really concern me, does it? If I recall, they're also excellent providers and good in bed."

He grinned, his teeth very white in the streetlights. "Smoking hot. Just ask Holly."

"I think I'll take your word for it. She might actually tell me, and I don't think I need the details."

He laughed as I followed his broad back up the stairs to our shared landing.

"Well, thanks again. I'll see you around."

He paused with his hand on his own front door. "You want to come in? I think we've got some leftover lasagne for dinner."

"No, I'm cool." I let myself into my apartment and looked around for Syl. There was no sign of her, but I hadn't really expected any. At the front door, I listened for a moment to make sure Joe had gone inside, then slipped out onto the empty landing again. Finally. I could hear the rumble of his deep voice talking to Holly behind the door of Number 1 as I headed back down the stairs. I wasn't interested in Lucas the werewolf. A certain fireshaper and his dodgy pet lion held all my attention right now.

Déjà vu. Here I was wandering through the dark bush again. At least it wasn't raining tonight. I trod lightly over the leaves and pebbles. No bushes rustled; not even a twig snapped as I passed. A cat padded silently alongside me—not Syl. This one was a ginger tomcat that I'd found and called to me as I left the road for the shelter of the trees. I wasn't going to waltz up the road to Steele's house and demand answers; I needed to be sneaky about this, so I'd slipped into the bush and circled round to approach the property from the rear.

I walked confidently, linked to the cat's senses, enjoying my enhanced abilities. My night vision was sharper, and I moved with more agility than normal, light on my feet. Cats were great for this sort of work. I'd used them many times in the city. More than predators, they were the ultimate sneaks—fast, quiet, and able to get into places no one could imagine.

It was cold, but I was moving fast enough to keep warm in my long black shirt and pants. The bush was alive with small creatures, and some not so small. I felt a wild deer passing off to my right somewhere, and the tiny minds of small rodents and the creatures that hunted them sparked in my inner sight, lighting up like the stars that hung overhead.

The moon was out too, only three or four nights from

full by the look of it. The darkness didn't bother me, and the moon was an old friend. I'd ranged under her light many a night before this, though usually my work had been done in dark alleys or across city rooftops, not out in the wild like this.

My companion and I slipped through the fence that marked the shaper's boundaries, and ghosted through the bush until the trees thinned and we found ourselves at the edge of his wide, rolling lawns. The house lay sprawled in the centre of its open space. Facing us was the long wall of glass, slightly fogged with moisture, that marked the location of his indoor pool. Beside it was the entry he'd led me through the night we'd staggered out of the bush with the two lost boys.

The lower storey was massive; the next level was only half the size, and each room seemed to boast a balcony. I could hardly enter through the door this time—the lawn in front of it was floodlit. I couldn't see into the dark rooms on the ground floor, but anyone inside would be able to see me.

I considered those balconies again. Most of them were just as exposed as the back entry, but a couple on the side had trees conveniently placed nearby, and the floodlights didn't cover that area. My companion and I circled around through the cover of the bush until we were opposite one of them.

I left the cat licking its paws under a flowering shrub and sprinted across the open space, feeling horribly exposed. I fetched up against the bole of a wide gum tree, heart hammering. No one shouted or shot at me, so I let out a deep breath and waited for my racing heart to calm.

The gum might have been more of a challenge to my unaugmented body, but linked to the cat I had no problem. I leapt off the ground and ran nimbly up the trunk, pausing to listen on a wide branch that overlooked the balcony. Still no alarms. I padded out along the branch and leapt down lightly onto the balcony. The door wasn't locked, so I slid it open and stepped inside, making sure to leave it open behind me in case I needed a quick exit later.

By the light of the moon, I could see enough of the room to guess I was in the shaper's bedroom, the one that Syl had been describing just before she disappeared. There was the bed, as enormous as she'd said. Surely half a dozen people could have slept comfortably in that monstrosity. Why on earth did he need a bed that big?

I pulled a small flashlight out of my pocket and moved silently across the carpet to another door. Beyond was a dressing room bigger than my whole bedroom. My flashlight swept across shirts, folded in neat colour-coordinated piles, rows of shoes, and an assortment of jeans hanging from the rail. Nothing that might give me a hint of why he was here, or where he had stashed Syl.

The other door off the bedroom concealed an en suite bathroom that boasted a marble spa bath and a shower big enough for ten. I closed that door and crept toward the one that opened into the hallway. I stood, listening and sending out my awareness, feeling within the house for any animal life that I could use.

Nothing. The house was quiet, so I slipped into the hall, moving slowly, checking each room that I passed. All were bedrooms or bathrooms, but none were occupied.

I halted at the top of the stairs and probed my link to Syl, just in case, but it was still silent. Dammit. Why couldn't she have been up here? Now I'd have to risk going downstairs. I set one foot on the top step. The staircase was wide and curved straight down to a marble foyer in front of imposing double doors. Outside those doors lay the driveway and the road to freedom. Inside was only mounting danger. Every step down that staircase left me more exposed. If someone came into the foyer, there would be nowhere to hide.

Now my black clothes were a hindrance. I stood out against the stark white walls like one rotten tooth in the middle of a smile. Only my fear for Syl drove me on.

My hearing, like my sight, was still augmented by my link to the ginger tom lurking outside in the bushes. I strained my ears for the slightest sound, jumpy as a cat on a hot tin roof. Two hallways led off the foyer. Down one I could hear voices, though I couldn't distinguish what they were saying, or even what gender they were. The sound was no more than a murmur behind closed doors. From my observations outside, I knew that the kitchen was down that way. To my right was only silence, so I chose that direction, stealing down the hall on nervous feet.

The first door was an office, with a laptop sitting on the large desk that dominated the room. I hesitated. It wasn't as good as finding Syl, but if I could discover what he was doing here ... Maybe just a quick peek. When I opened the laptop with my gloved fingers, the screen lit up. Excellent. He was still logged in. No messing around with passwords.

I set my flashlight down on the desk and considered the glowing screen. Where to start? Emails would probably bear the quickest fruit, but which might tell me something about his motives for coming here? It could be any of them.

Best to just start at the top and check the most recent. As I scanned down the list my gaze fell on a name I recognised and my blood ran cold.

Erik Anders.

Those cold dark eyes. The cruel twist to that mouth, which only smiled at someone else's misfortune.

"I need you to acquire this," he'd said, as expressionless as if he'd just asked me to pass the sugar.

I still remembered the shock that had burned through my body, leaving me cold and shaking in its wake.

"You mean steal it," I'd said, barely managing to control the tremor in my voice. How could he possibly expect me to break into the home of the First Councillor, the famous Ruby Adept, and steal something? It was a death sentence if I was caught.

"It doesn't belong to him anyway," he'd said, as if that made it all right.

I'd stared into those cold eyes and realised it was a death sentence regardless. Whether I did it or not, whether I succeeded or not, there was no happy ending for me in this story.

If I failed, the Ruby Adept would kill me.

And if I succeeded … Erik Anders would. He couldn't leave me free to tell of what I'd done. I might as well put a gun to my head on the spot and save myself some trouble.

"It'll cost you," I'd said, desperate to find a way out, a way that didn't end with me dead in an alley somewhere. I couldn't say no, now that he'd told me what he wanted. That way ended in the alley, too. But if I bargained and made him think I was taking the job, that might buy me enough time to make a run for it.

His lip had curled. "Name your price."

I'd picked an outrageous sum. Predictably, he'd counter-offered something pathetic, and we'd settled in to bargain in earnest, while nervous sweat ran down between my breasts and soaked the fabric of my shirt.

Why was Steele corresponding with Anders? They were both on the council, so maybe it wasn't unusual, though Anders was only junior compared to Steele. His secondary element was water, which was odd for a fireshaper. Fire and water were such opposites, the two sides of his power warred against each other, weakening both. Normally such a shaper wouldn't be considered for a council seat, but he had plenty of the right kind of friends, so he'd finally managed to slime his way in. His email could be nothing more than two councillors discussing council business.

The subject line said "Re: Stolen altarpiece". That made my heart sink almost as much as the name of the sender. I clicked to open it, and that was when the lights flicked on.

Steele stood in the doorway, hand still on the light switch. "By the gods!"

I leapt up, shoving the chair back violently, but before I could even take a step a ring of fire leapt up around the desk.

His eyes narrowed. For a fireshaper, he had one hell of a chilly expression on his face.

"How did you get in here? And what in the name of Apollo are you doing with my laptop?"

I faced him, trembling in spite of myself. What could I say? There was no way to explain this. Talk about caught red-handed. I'd had some close shaves in my time slipping in and out of other people's houses, but I'd never been caught like this. The shock of the email had focused my attention so much that I hadn't heard him approach.

I licked dry lips and stared at him across the dancing

flames. Was it my imagination or was the circle of fire shrinking around me, moving closer? "I'm … I'm looking for my cat."

He folded muscular arms across his chest and leaned against the doorframe. I wasn't fooled by his casual stance. A muscle jumped in his jaw, as if he was clenching his teeth.

"I doubt your cat is hiding in my laptop." Yep, he was pissed. All the stories I'd heard about shaper "justice" nagged at the back of my mind, turning my knees to water. "Why are you in my house?"

I said nothing. The wall of flame in front of me pushed closer. Definitely not my imagination. I stepped back and the flames followed. Gradually the ring of fire herded me away from the desk until I stood in the centre of the room, tightly encircled. I was sweating hard, the heat of the flames uncomfortable on my skin.

He moved to the desk chair I'd just vacated and dropped into it. His gaze flicked to the laptop screen, checking to see what I'd been looking at, then back up to me. Flames danced in his eyes as he leaned back and waved a languid hand.

"I can keep this up all night, you know."

I just bet he could. That bed upstairs spoke of a certain dedication. But right now his sexual prowess was of less interest to me than his control of his shaping. Those flames were hot.

"You're going to tell me what you are. Right now." The flames licked closer, and I shut my eyes. "It would be a shame to damage that pretty face. Are you a new kind of shadow? But whose?"

I had no idea what he was talking about. Someone's shadow? He was making no sense.

He slammed his hand down on the desk, and I jumped. "Answer me! Don't think I won't hurt you, because I will. I don't care what Alberto says. You've obviously managed to fool him. Why can't I sense your shaping energy?"

"I don't *have* any shaping energy." My face prickled with heat, beads of sweat forming on my upper lip. "I'm not a shaper."

"Then how did you find those boys?" There was no mercy on his face. No humanity at all.

My heart beat a frightened rhythm against my ribs. He would kill me, and then who would help Syl?

"I just … have a knack." It was lame, but I had to say something. His anger was terrifying. I would have told him anything to make him drop those flames, if only I'd had the faintest idea what he wanted to hear. "I've always been good at finding things."

"Yet you can't find your cat. So much for your knack." His muscles were tense, like a spring coiled to break free. "I assume this is the little cat shifter I saw in the bookshop?"

I said nothing, which answered his question. His lip

curved into a sardonic smile. How had he known Syl was a shifter, when not even the other shifters in town could tell? She'd buried her humanity so deep.

I could feel my skin scorching, and the acrid smell of singed hair made my eyes water. Anger welled up inside me, deep and fierce, burning away my fear. He was as bad as Anders.

"Why are you looking for her here?" Flames flickered in his eyes, the reflection of the flames that danced around me, ready to kill me on his whim.

That was another question I couldn't answer. *Because she was here spying on you when she went missing? Because someone attacked her and I thought it might be you?* I was ready to believe him capable of anything. Bastard. The air around me was so hot it hurt to breathe. I reached out to the glittering web of life that surrounded the house, hunting for something that might help me, but the closest thing was the ginger tom I'd brought with me. I urged him up the tree and across to the balcony door that I'd left open.

He sighed. "You're wasting my time. You could at least have come up with a better excuse. Looking for your cat." He snorted and got to his feet in a lithe movement. He moved like a shifter himself, a panther maybe. He stopped just the other side of the flames. I could have reached out and touched him if I hadn't minded getting crisped. "Tell me what you're really looking for, or your cat won't be the only one missing."

He loomed closer, and I shrank back as far as the flames permitted, trying to get him between me and the door. I was only partially successful, but with all his attention on me he wasn't likely to notice a small cat.

"It's awfully hot in here." I unbuttoned the top two buttons of my shirt. It was hard to act sexy when I felt like a chicken on a rotisserie. It was even harder to pretend I felt anything other than deepest hatred for him right then, but those flames were a powerful motivator. The fabric of my shirt clung to me, damp with sweat, and I pulled it away from my skin, fanning myself with one hand. "Why don't you drop these flames and we can talk about this like civilised people?"

"Or like one civilised person and one traitor," he growled, and he stepped through the flames as if they weren't there.

I moved closer, until the heat of his body rivalled the heat of the flames. His eyes flicked to my exposed cleavage, but there was no mercy in them when he met my gaze again. His burning need for answers was the only thing keeping me alive now, and I licked my lips nervously. Flames danced in his eyes. He was almost where I wanted him; I just needed him to turn a little bit … that way.

What I needed was a diversion and, despite that brief look, he wasn't falling for my seduction routine. In desperation, I leapt toward him, plastering myself against him, and dragged his face down for a kiss.

It certainly wasn't the greatest kiss I'd ever had. He froze in surprise for a moment, his mouth soft under mine, then thrust me away. *Rejected by the fireshaper*—it sounded like one of the titles from the romance shelves in the bookshop. In real life it was damn embarrassing. But his flames had sunk low—almost gone out—with the unexpectedness of my move, so I was calling that a win.

I summoned the cat as Steele glared at me, nonplussed. It streaked into the room like a ginger rocket, leaping and clawing its way up his body. He swung around, shouting. The flames snuffed out completely as he lost his concentration. The cat yowled, clinging to the back of Steele's head as he groped for it. If this had been a romance this scene would have ended very differently.

Since it wasn't, I shoved him hard in the back and leapt for the door.

I flew along the hallway back to the foyer. The taste of him was still on my lips, and my cheeks were bright with embarrassment. Clearly, "temptress" wasn't going on my resumé any time soon. The look on his face as he'd flung me away made me squirm.

Behind me there was a sudden roar of flame and my link to the ginger cat was abruptly severed. I thrust the almost-kiss from my mind and cast my net wide, searching for allies. Charging through a door at the back of the foyer, I found a long, high-ceilinged room. This end was a sitting area, like a family room. Down the other end was a billiards table and a bar, and through the archway I could see the pool waters lit from below, gleaming a bright blue, still and inviting.

A man lay on one of the couches. He didn't stir as I ran past. It was the lion shifter, apparently still sleeping off the effects of Alberto's attack. Shifters had great regenerative powers, but they needed food and sleep to work. Steele had dumped him on the white couch with no regard for the blood that covered his clothes. Whoever had to clean the upholstery wasn't going to be happy, but I was guessing that wouldn't be Steele.

I skidded to a stop at the glass doors that lined the back wall of the room and wrenched open the nearest one. Cool night air hit me in the face as I plunged down the steps and ran across the wide lawn towards the safety of the trees, my shadow stretching out before me. I borrowed a distant owl's night vision to keep myself from losing my footing in the dark.

I was almost at the tree line when a fireball whizzed past and exploded in the treetops, lighting up the night with orange flame. I yelped and tried to move faster, though I was already running at full stretch. Another fireball landed closer; its heat warmed my face. My heart pounded as my legs and arms pumped desperately.

A wall of flame erupted in front of me, cutting me off from the trees. I turned, searching wildly for sanctuary, but Steele was nearly on me and there was nowhere to run. I was caught, back to the leaping flames, like an animal brought to bay.

He stalked toward me across the lawn. The night was alive with fire, sending dark shadows writhing across the grass between us. Blood ran down his face from a scratch above his eyes, and there was more blood matted in his hair. His smile was almost feral.

"Another friend of yours?" he asked, stopping just out of reach. "You do seem to know a lot of cats."

"You killed it."

"I killed it. Or did you? You were controlling it somehow, weren't you? Cats don't just attack people out of the blue like that."

I swallowed hard. That steely glint was back in his eye, and I was fresh out of options. My unbuttoned shirt had lost whatever meagre attraction it had held; Steele's expression was all business again, and there was nothing bigger than a bush rat within call.

"Maybe that cat was just a great judge of character. You're going to burn us out if you don't shut that fire down." I was proud of how calm I sounded.

He waved an impatient hand and the flames fell away to nothing. Then that same hand shot out and grabbed my arm. The contact burned into me, and I gasped.

He dragged me close. "Last chance, Lexi. Tell me who sent you."

"No one." I held his fiery gaze, tilting my head to look up at him. "I told you, I came here to find Syl. I know she's in danger."

He didn't look convinced. "Why look here? Why assume it was me? It's a big town. She could be anywhere."

The smell of smoke filled my nostrils. I could feel the distress and confusion among the nearby creatures. That smell meant danger.

"Because you're new." This man meant danger, too, but I was already up to my neck in trouble. Couldn't get much deeper. "Everything was fine until you arrived. Did you take her?"

He laughed, a sneering sound. "So protective! What are you going to do? Set another kitty cat on me?"

I lifted my chin. The bastard needn't think he could be condescending.

"Afraid?"

"You caught me by surprise, that's all." His grip on my arm was like iron. "You won't get lucky like that again."

"If you had nothing to do with it, why did she disappear the minute you showed up?"

A thoughtful look appeared in his eyes. Well, that was an improvement on naked fury. He was silent for a long moment. When he spoke again, he sounded much calmer.

"You know, it's not polite to read other people's emails." He caught my wrist and marched me back toward the house. "Particularly if you have to break into their home to do it."

The long white room dazzled my eyes after the darkness outside. Steele shut the glass door firmly behind us and frowned down at me.

"I'm not the only stranger in town. Let's ask Mason if he's seen your little cat shifter."

He turned toward the couch, and it was only then that I noticed the lion shifter was no longer lying on it. He'd left some lovely blood stains, so it was definitely the right couch, but there was no sign of the body that had been passed out there only moments before.

Steele's frown deepened as he towed me through the door into the foyer.

"Mason? Are you there?"

So now Steele knew his name? In the bar he'd acted like he had no idea who the guy was. Why had he pretended he didn't know him? What was he trying to hide?

A car started up in the driveway, and Steele hauled me toward the front door. We got there in time to see taillights, gleaming red, disappear around the first bend in the road.

"Is that him?" I asked, then felt like an idiot. Fireshaping didn't come with X-ray vision, as far as I knew. "Where's he going?"

An equally stupid question, but all Steele said was: “Let’s find out, shall we?”

He hurried me to the garage, which was a freestanding building to one side of the main house. Inside, a red convertible stood alone in the cavernous space, all gleaming curves and sleek, powerful lines.

“Get in.” He pushed me toward the passenger side. “He’s taken the limo. Shouldn’t be too hard to catch.”

He started the car and backed out. It was small, only big enough for two, but the engine throbbed with power. It smelled of leather and luxury. We roared down the driveway, my hair streaming behind me until I caught it into a hasty knot at the nape of my neck.

“North or south?” I asked. North was the big city lights of Crosston, but perhaps he’d go south instead, expecting us to choose the more likely road north.

Steele didn’t take either direction at the turn-off to the highway. Instead he headed into town.

“I doubt he’ll leave straight away. The limo’s too conspicuous. He’ll want his own car.”

He turned into the first motel on Marine Parade and did a circuit of the parking lot. No sign of the limo. Back on the road, he headed for the next motel, just around the corner, and repeated the procedure.

“This is a tourist town,” I said. “Plenty of places to stay besides motels. He could be anywhere.”

He raised one eyebrow. “Are you always so positive? Just keep your eyes peeled for the limo.”

If I was negative, didn’t I have reason? Life hadn’t exactly been a picnic, unlike his no doubt luxurious existence. Fuming, I looked away and sent my awareness out instead, enlisting other eyes to aid the search. The limo should be easy to spot. You didn’t see too many of those in Berkley’s Bay. We were a little too laid-back for the limo crowd.

A rat turned up something that looked promising. “Try the Star, on Fulton Street.”

He cast me a curious glance.

Belatedly I added, “They have the best rooms. Lions like their luxuries.”

I doubted he believed my hasty excuse, but the little sports car zipped around the corner and we were soon pulling into the parking lot of the Star, one of the more upmarket motels in Berkley’s Bay. As we passed the office, a white sedan zipped past us going the other way. I saw a flash of blonde hair in the lights from the office, and then the car was gone in a screech of tyres.

“That was him!”

Steele spun the wheel and set out in pursuit. Mason was heading for the highway and he wasn’t bothering himself with the speed limit. The white car squealed around the corner into the main street. Just as well it was late at night and no one was on the crossing, because he would have run them down. He swerved around a lone car that was doing a sensible speed and roared down the street.

I clutched my seat as Steele overtook the same car. "Try not to kill us."

He flashed me a grin, his hands relaxed on the wheel. He was actually enjoying this. "You want your friend back or not?"

I couldn't argue with that so I kept my mouth shut and held on tight. We'd come to the long straight stretch just before the road went into a series of sharp bends. The turn-off to the highway was just beyond that. Steele put his foot down, and the distance between the two cars closed rapidly. The road was climbing now, and the shifter's car obviously didn't have the same power under the bonnet as the red convertible.

We topped the rise, only a couple of car lengths behind him now, and closing rapidly. The first bend was approaching and I glanced at Steele uneasily. He still looked as relaxed as if he were out for a nice Sunday afternoon drive, and showed no sign of slowing down for the corner.

Mason took the corner at high speed. His back wheels fishtailed out to the side, but he managed to get the car back under control. We flew around the corner right behind him, the low-slung sports car gripping the road securely.

Trees flashed by in the light from the headlights, disappearing into the dark behind us. Only two more bends before the highway. Which way would he go?

"Are we going to drive like this all the way to Crosston?" I asked, still holding on for dear life.

"If we have to." He glanced at me, his face unreadable. "I could blow him up now if you'd prefer."

"Not if Syl's in there!" It was too dark to see if anyone else was in the car. He might even have left her at the motel. We hadn't had time to check. Of course, that was assuming Steele was even right about him taking her in the first place. And assuming that Steele wasn't lying through his teeth. Those were some big assumptions right there.

He and Mason obviously knew each other. But why had Mason stolen his car and taken off like that, if they were on the same side?

"Why did you act like you had no idea who your friend Mason was at the pub?"

He threw me a brief glare. "He's no friend of mine."

Okay, bad choice of words. Friends didn't usually steal each other's limousines. "But you know him. You can't deny that."

Steele edged the sports car closer. For a moment I had visions of him ramming the other car, the way they did in movies, but apparently he had more respect for his car's bodywork.

"If you start asking questions you might have to answer a few yourself. What's so special about your little cat friend that Mason wants her?"

"I have no idea. I've never seen him before in my life." But if he was the one who'd surprised Syl earlier, then obviously *she* had. I'd felt the shock of recognition as she'd said, *What is* he *doing here?* Of course I'd only known Syl for a year, so I didn't know all the people she was acquainted with. Maybe he was a long-lost cousin. But I doubted it. "As far as I know, there's nothing special about Syl at all. How do you know this guy? Who is he?"

"No one. An enforcer."

We were all but sitting on the white car's bumper bar, and the next bend was coming up fast. I braced my feet against the front wall and clutched the seat even tighter.

"An enforcer for who? One of your council buddies? Is that why you're protecting him?"

He smiled, a dangerous baring of teeth that gleamed white in the darkness. "You think I'm protecting him? I'm about to run him off the road."

It all happened so quickly. The white car took the bend, tyres squealing. The back slid out again and the tyres left the bitumen, spewing out great clouds of dust and pebbles. The car spun, the driver fighting for control, then slammed into a tree.

The noise was immense. Steele pulled up further down

the road, and I was out of the car before it had even come to a complete stop, running back toward the wreck in the dark. Smoke poured from under the bonnet and glass lay shattered all over the road, sparkling in the moon's faint light. The car itself was wrapped around the tree, the front passenger side completely obliterated. The remaining headlight lit the branches above, tilted up at a crazy angle. A hole gaped where the windscreen had been.

Mason had been thrown clear—apparently, he hadn't got the memo about wearing his seatbelt. As I approached, he rose to his feet, shaking his head groggily, and staggered into the darkness beneath the trees. A fireball chased him, setting the night ablaze.

I had no time to waste on him. I ran to the car. "Steele! Leave him!"

Steele turned at my call, letting the fire that blazed from his palms die down.

"Help me get this door open!" I tugged at the back door of the wreck, but it was bent out of shape and wouldn't budge.

He strode over and laid his hands on the edges of the door, gently nudging me out of the way with his hip. Under his hands the metal glowed molten and he dug his fingers into and *through* the door, melting and shaping it. His muscles strained as he planted his feet and heaved. I forgot my dislike of him, and my suspicion that he was somehow working with Anders, and pressed close, willing him to hurry. A ticking sound came from somewhere under the crumpled bonnet, and the engine smelled of hot oil.

The door popped off and he hurled it aside. On the back seat lay a woman in dirty running gear, a woman I knew well but hadn't seen in many months.

Sylvie.

10

She looked to be no more than sleeping. No wonder our link had gone dead—it only worked when she was in her animal form. Her chest rose and fell in even breaths, but when I shook her she didn't wake.

"Syl!" I shook her harder. "Wake up!"

"She's probably drugged," Steele said.

He sounded so casual, as if this was an everyday occurrence. Drugged? Why would this Mason guy kidnap Syl, force her into human form—because it was highly unlikely Syl would have shifted of her own volition—and then drug her? Where was he taking her?

Out here, alone in the dark with Jake Steele, with the only sounds that ominous ticking from under the wrecked car's bonnet and the faint crackle of flame in the bushes at the side of the road, I suddenly felt horribly exposed. Yet I couldn't keep my mouth shut. The way he'd said *She's probably drugged*, as if it didn't matter either way, made me want to punch him in the throat.

"This is your fault!"

"Mine?" He leaned into the wrecked car and eased Syl out, gentle despite his apparent lack of concern. "How do you figure that?"

"She was taken from your house, by a guy you pretended not to know but obviously do." I was ninety-nine per cent sure that was how it had happened, anyway. "And you were pretty quick to hide him away from Alberto and everyone else."

"Alberto would have drained him dry. Just because I saved the guy's arse doesn't make him my best buddy. And it certainly doesn't make me responsible for his kidnapping attempts. Do you think I would have chased after him to get her back if he was working for me?"

Sylvie's head lolled against his shoulder, her dark hair loose around her face. It was longer than last time I'd seen it. A small gash on her cheek was closing already, thanks to her shifter powers of regeneration. Hopefully there were no internal injuries, but her body should be able to deal with those, too. If it couldn't, there'd be nothing any doctor could do for her anyway. Shifter healing powers were so good that shifters could recover from almost anything; if they didn't, the injury wasn't survivable by any means.

"Why did you, then? One minute you're trying to

barbecue me, the next you're playing white knight? I'm not buying it."

"Sweetheart, I'm not trying to sell you anything." His tone was weary, tinged with annoyance. "The guy was interfering with a council investigation. Now get back in the car."

"Why should I?" *Council investigation*. I didn't like the sound of that. Come to think of it, I wasn't too keen on the *sweetheart* either.

"So I can dump your friend in your lap and drive you both back to town. Or were you planning on carrying her back there yourself? Because I'm not. For a cat, she weighs a lot."

Somewhat mollified, I got in, and he settled Syl on my lap. "What are you investigating? It can't have anything to do with Syl, whatever it is."

He waved a casual hand at the small brush fires flickering at the margins of the bush lining the road, and they all went out as if doused by a shower of cold water. I drew a deep breath, reminded of just whom I was talking to, and what he was capable of.

He looked across at me as he started the car. "Can't it? You seem to know a lot for a girl who works in a second-hand bookshop. Maybe you can assist me."

I watched him out of the corner of my eye as he drove. He had a face straight off the cover of a romance novel:

strong jaw, straight nose, and those piercing eyes that looked right through you without giving away what he was thinking. In other circumstances, sitting in an expensive sports car with a man like that would be a dream come true.

I tightened my arms around my unconscious friend. In these circumstances, it was more like a nightmare. He kept sidestepping the issue of his connection to Mason, and now he was implying Syl was the subject of a council investigation? Syl, of all people?

"Syl doesn't do anything except sit on a cushion in the bookshop all day. Last time I checked, that wasn't a crime."

"Well, that's a relief. The mayor seems convinced there's a gang of cat shifters on a rampage through town—and now I discover a cat shifter who's hiding the fact she's a shifter. You can see how that looks suspicious."

His tone was all sweetness. I jostled Syl's head into a more comfortable position against my shoulder and glared at him.

"A *gang* of cat shifters?"

"Yes, apparently several of them ransacked his house last week. He was most insistent that they should be brought to justice. As Master of the South-East, that job falls to me."

My heart sank. Syl had been right; I should never have stolen Johnson's damn altarpiece.

Steele's sarcastic tone told me what he thought of Johnson's claims, but he *had* come to investigate, hadn't he? And he'd obviously mentioned the altarpiece to Anders. I wished I'd had time to read that email. Had Anders guessed that the thief might be someone he was looking for? The mention of cats had probably tipped him off. If he'd sent this Mason guy out looking, it was time to pack our bags.

"As Master of the South-East, I would have thought you'd be too busy to investigate every petty little break-and-enter. I guess we can all sleep safe in our beds now, knowing that you're here to protect us."

He threw me an amused glance, but said nothing. Cramming Syl onto my lap for the ride back to town in the little sports car was neither comfortable nor safe, but at least it was over quickly. I unlocked the street door to my apartment block then stood aside for Steele to carry her up the stairs. It was after two in the morning and I should have been exhausted, but my body still buzzed with adrenaline.

The dim bulb on the landing cast soft shadows as I unlocked the door to my apartment, conscious of the shaper behind me. The landing was small and I could feel the heat he radiated. Any minute now that banked fire could burst into flame. I didn't trust him one bit not to direct those flames at me. The link between him, Erik Anders, and the mysterious Mr Mason loomed like a giant, foreboding question mark in my mind. If he hadn't been carrying Syl, I could happily have shoved him down the stairs.

As it was I let him in and showed him to Syl's room. My tiny apartment looked ridiculous, like a little dolls' house, after the luxurious expanses of his home. There was barely room to walk between the lounge and the kitchen bench to get to the short hallway that led to the bedrooms and bathroom. The day's dishes were still on the sink where I'd left them to drain, and the lounge room looked, as usual, like an explosion in a library, with books and magazines scattered on every flat surface. The rip in the arm of the old leather couch was normally covered by a throw, but at the moment that was puddled on the carpet under an open magazine.

He made no comment as he carried Syl through. Her room was super neat by comparison to the rest of the apartment—no clothes on the floor or personal belongings scattered about. The bed was always made because Syl slept on top of it. He laid her gently on top of the quilt.

"What now?" I asked as we both looked at her unconscious form. "Are you arresting her?"

He cast me an impatient look. "I have more pressing concerns right now than the Mayor's dramas. I'll talk to you both tomorrow."

That was it? No accusations of shifter gang rampages? No more questions about my failed break-in at his house? He was just going to leave?

"I'll look forward to it," I said.

He raised an eyebrow at my sarcastic tone. "So will I."

The way he let his eyes roam over my body as he spoke brought a flush of heat to my cheeks. That was probably his revenge for my abortive seduction attempt earlier. I marched to the front door and pointedly held it open, trying to ignore the fact that my shirt still gaped open from when I'd unbuttoned it. He laughed as he stepped onto the landing.

I shut the door behind him, a little more forcefully than necessary. It seemed as though all his anger and suspicion at me had been diverted to Mason instead. He'd made some connection that I couldn't see.

Steele was a puzzle, but not one I was interested in solving. He was altogether too powerful, and had the wrong kind of connections.

I peeked in on Syl, but she hadn't moved, so I jumped into the shower. It had been a long night.

As I turned my face up to the hot water, an unexpected lump formed in my throat. We'd only been here a few months, but I didn't want to leave. Yet how could we stay? If Anders didn't know where we were already, he would as soon as he heard from Mason. Syl and I needed to be far away before he turned up.

Through the noise of the shower I thought I heard something else. Was Syl awake? I shut off the water and stepped out, reaching for my towel. Someone was knocking on the door.

Who the hell would be knocking on my door at nearly three o'clock in the morning? I hesitated. It was probably Steele. He'd decided to arrest me after all. But I wasn't going to greet him wringing wet and wrapped in a towel. Not after our earlier interlude.

I marched into the lounge room. "Who's there?"

"Lexi, it's me, Holly."

Immediately my thoughts leapt to the baby, and I flung the door open. "Are you all right? Is the baby coming?"

She stepped inside and smiled, not a very cheerful smile. "No, I'm fine. Still got a couple of weeks to wait. You're dripping all over the carpet. Did I get you out of the shower? Sorry."

"That's okay. What's wrong?"

She shrugged. "You tell me. Jake Steele came banging on our door a few minutes ago. Demanded that Joe go with him to look for some guy. Said he needed a tracker."

"Oh." So he'd decided to hunt down Mason. That was interesting. I wished I knew what Steele was really doing in town. He hadn't sounded as though he took the Mayor's claims too seriously, yet here he was.

I waved her to the couch. "Have a seat. I'll just go and put some clothes on."

Someone yawned and I froze halfway across the room. Holly looked at me enquiringly.

"Have you got someone here?" I could see her putting

two and two together as she flushed. Clearly my standing here naked in a towel looked different now. "I'm sorry, I didn't mean to interrupt. I was just worried about where he was taking Joe."

"It's okay." I held out a hand to stop her as she turned to the door. Joe and Holly were my best friends in this place. Perhaps in all the world, now, except for Syl. I was going to have to get mighty creative to explain why Steele had turned up on their doorstep at this time of night. He'd obviously implicated me in some way already or she wouldn't be here. It might just be easier to tell her the truth. After all, this might be the last time I would ever see her.

A pang of sorrow pierced me at that thought. I'd never get to see the baby either. "Come in. It's just Syl."

She raised an eyebrow. That hadn't sounded like a cat's yawn. But she followed me to the door of Syl's bedroom.

Curled up in the middle of the quilt, her tail tucked around her nose, lay a small black cat.

"You found her, then? Joe said she'd gone missing."

I stared as Syl showed her pink tongue in another yawn.

Anyone would think you'd never seen a cat before, she said. **Shut your mouth before you catch a fly.**

What the hell, Syl? You were human a second ago. Human, and unconscious. Are you all right?

Nothing a good night's sleep won't fix. She put her head back down and shut her eyes.

"I'll just get dressed," I said to Holly. "Back in a sec."

When I came back out Holly was still standing in Syl's doorway, frowning at the sleeping cat.

"Something seems different about her. What's wrong with her?"

"Nothing." I took Holly's elbow and tried to turn her back toward the lounge room, but she wouldn't budge. "Maybe she was in a fight. She seems pretty tired."

Holly took a step into the room. I could tell Syl was only pretending to be asleep. Holly's nose twitched, and she sniffed the air suspiciously.

Her eyes widened, and she turned to me in shock. "She's a shifter!"

Now the cat's out of the bag, Syl grumbled.

I didn't know what to say. Holly looked gutted.

"All this time! Why didn't you tell us?" Then a puzzled frown crossed her brow. "And how come we couldn't tell?"

The cat stared back at her, blinking her green eyes slowly, and then she shimmered into a slender woman who uncurled herself and stood up. "Jeez, it's cold without fur."

I gave Holly a gentle push toward the lounge room, and this time she went.

"I don't understand," she said. "I've seen that cat every day since you arrived. I never once suspected. Has she been in cat form the whole time?"

I nodded and her eyes widened.

"But why?"

"Because we came here to get away from someone. Berkley's Bay is nice and quiet." At least, it had been. If only that damn Steele hadn't come to town. "It seemed as far as we could get from Crosston and still be in shaper territory."

Syl walked back in, dragging one of my sweaters over her head. Holly stared at her unashamedly, shaking her head.

"I still can't believe … Is your name really Sylvie?"

"Sure. Sylvie Wentworth." Syl stuck out her hand and shook with the bemused werewolf.

"I thought about christening her Pumpkin or Fluffikins, but she would have made my life hell," I added dryly.

Syl plonked herself on the couch next to me and put her bare feet in my lap. Cat people weren't very good at respecting other people's boundaries. But I was so pleased to see her in human form that I didn't care.

"Who are you hiding from? Steele? Why are you running around with him in the middle of the night?"

Syl and I exchanged glances. We could no longer communicate telepathically, but I knew what she was thinking. *Should we tell her?* I nodded. It wouldn't make much difference now, and Holly deserved to know the reason why before we disappeared.

"There's a shaper in Crosston," Syl said. "Erik Anders. Have you heard of him?"

Holly shook her head. That wasn't surprising. Crosston was a big place, and there were a lot of shapers there.

"He's not very strong," I said. "He's got a water secondary. But he's on the council now."

"And he's crooked as a dog's hind leg," Syl added.

Yes, well, weren't they all? I wouldn't trust a shaper as far as I could throw him. They were all too used to having the world ordered to suit themselves, and didn't take kindly to opposition.

"He wanted us to steal something for him." I glossed over this part. I didn't want to explain why I was such an ideal candidate for the job. "We said no, and he didn't take it very well."

"He set fire to our whole apartment block," Syl said bleakly.

Had everyone escaped the fire? We didn't even know.

Holly drew in a shocked breath. "He did that because you said no?"

I sighed. "He did that so that we wouldn't tell anyone what he'd asked us to do. He meant for us to die in the fire. But we escaped."

"And you've been hiding from him ever since?"

"That's right," I said.

"But why would it be so terrible if you told anyone?"

"I'd tell you, but then I'd have to kill you." I smiled weakly, but it didn't sound funny even to me. "Let's just say there are powerful people involved, and leave it at that. But I think he's found us."

Holly was quick to catch on. "Does this have something to do with what Steele and Joe are doing?"

I nodded. "Yes. Pretty sure."

Her eyes filled with fear. "Is Joe safe?"

I hurried to reassure her. "I'm sure he's fine. That lion shifter guy—you know the one from the pub that Alberto attacked? He took Syl. Steele and I went after him, but he got away. Steele's trying to get Joe to help track him down."

"Oh. He said something about a lion, but I was only half awake. Why did the lion guy take Syl?"

"He works for Anders," Syl said. "His name's Parker Mason."

Oh, hell. Having my suspicions confirmed opened a pit of anxiety in my stomach. "How do you know him?"

"I'd seen him around a few times—before you came to the city. He used to hire out to anyone who needed muscle, but then he got a gig with Anders."

"I never saw him."

"I think he travelled a bit. Anders has his fingers in pies all over the country. And you weren't with us that long before ..." She trailed off. *Before the fire.*

"Why does Steele care that this Mason guy tried to abduct Syl?" Holly asked. "Shapers don't usually bother themselves with what the shifters get up to."

"I think they're working together," Syl said, and there

was real fear in her eyes. "I was at Steele's house when Mason grabbed me."

I wasn't so sure. It was me Anders really wanted. Taking Syl was just the bait to lure me. Steele could have taken me any time tonight if he'd wanted to, but instead he'd helped get Syl back.

"That's bad," Holly said.

You could say that again. Even if he wasn't in league with Anders, Steele was a powerful shaper. Just because he hadn't incinerated me the minute he found me snooping in his study, it didn't mean I could trust him. I wasn't sticking around to have that conversation with him tomorrow. I couldn't take the risk. Our lives were on the line.

"We'll have to run," Syl said.

Holly didn't argue, though her eyes were bright with tears. I felt a little teary myself. I'd miss her and Joe, their pretend fights and their easy acceptance. Even Joe's stupid jokes about Lucas. It didn't matter to them that I wasn't a wolf. They'd been prepared to welcome me into their lives. And now I'd have to leave them and Alberto and Tegan behind, and start again somewhere else.

"Do you need money?" Holly asked.

"No." As if I could take her money, with a baby coming and no job. But it was like her to offer. "We'll be fine."

There was one thing I had to do before we left, though. I had to say goodbye to Alberto.

11

I'm coming with you, Syl said, sticking to my heels like a shadow as I hurried down the stairs. She hadn't stayed long in her human form once Holly had left.

"I won't be long. You could stay here and start packing."

It's all your stuff anyway. Pack your own shit. I'm not hanging around here on my own, wondering if some other old friend is going to turn up and smash me over the head.

"Is that what he did?" She'd never actually told me how he'd managed to capture her. Now I felt guilty that I hadn't checked her over a little more carefully—though, in my defence, shifters were fast healers.

The cold night air hit me in the face as we left the building and jogged across the street to the pub. The place was deserted: no cars parked outside, no drinkers loitering on the pavement. It was way past closing time.

No.* Syl's mental voice sounded bitter. **Bastard shot me with a tranquiliser dart.

I frowned down at her as I rattled the door of the pub. Locked. Your garden-variety thug didn't normally come equipped with tranq guns. That sounded horribly prepared. It was looking more and more likely that Steele had tipped off Anders to our presence. Possibly unintentionally.

I couldn't quite understand why Steele was off chasing the lion shifter now if they were on the same side, but I was prepared to believe anything of shapers. Most likely, it was just a falling out among thieves. At least it gave us a chance to skip town before Steele came knocking in the morning.

Regardless, it was clear our friend Mason hadn't come to Berkley's Bay because he'd heard it was a great place to kick back and take the sea air. Syl had been right. I should never have taken that damn altarpiece.

I hammered on the door. Alberto was probably still in there, and he wouldn't be asleep at this time. I guess he could be out, doing whatever vampires do in the dark hours before dawn. I'd never enquired as to Alberto's sustenance, but there'd been no suspicious disappearances since I'd come to town, so I figured he managed without causing too much damage. I didn't believe those rumours of the captive blood donors in the cellar. That just didn't jibe with the person I knew. The townspeople seemed to like him well enough, which also made it seem unlikely that he was a murderous, bloodsucking demon. But then, some people would do anything for free beer.

The door creaked open and Alberto's pale face appeared in the gloom between the outer and inner doors.

"I assume you're not here for a drink, because I closed hours ago." He gestured impatiently as I hesitated on the doorstep. "Come in, come in, you're letting out all the warm air."

I followed him in. He was cute like that, pretending that warm air meant anything to him. He had such a knack of blending in that I often forgot he was a vampire at all. Until he did something like attacking Mason the other night. Those swirling shadows had sure been something else. It made me wonder whether some of the more outlandish claims about him were true after all. If he could suck all the light from the room like that, what else could he do? Maybe he really could turn into smoke and disappear through a keyhole, or call nightmare creatures out of the ground.

He waited until I'd closed the outer door behind me before opening the inner door, even though there was no damaging UV radiation outside at this time of night. But he was very strict about his door protocol, and even his drunkest customers soon learned the rules.

Inside, the lights were dimmer than usual, with most turned off apart from the ones over the massive wooden bar. I was used to seeing the place full of people. It seemed less cosy without the roar of conversation and laughter filling it. The shadows pressed in, seeping out of the corners and creeping into the rest of the room.

"I'm here to say goodbye." Although if he did happen to offer a drink, I wouldn't say no. It had been that kind of day.

One finely arched eyebrow arched even higher. Alberto looked like a caricature of a vampire, with his dark hair swept back from his forehead, his fine features, his rather autocratic nose and sensual lips. When he pulled that quizzical expression, he brought to mind every corny actor who'd ever played Dracula. I sometimes wondered if his maker had chosen him simply because he looked like a man born to be a vampire.

"You're leaving town? Why?"

Syl stalked past and leapt up onto the bar, where she perched like a sphinx surveying her domain.

"Something bad has happened."

He glanced at the cat, her tail idly twitching behind her. "I gathered that, if it managed to goose Sylvie right out of her cat skin. But what, exactly?"

The tail stilled. I could feel Syl's shock through our link. I stared at him, not knowing what to say. And then I remembered the stories about what happened to people who got caught in a vampire's hypnotic gaze, and dropped my eyes, just to be safe.

He tapped the bar impatiently with one long elegant finger. “Come now, ladies, let’s not pretend. I’ve known ever since you showed up on my doorstep that Sylvie is a shifter. I saw no reason to pry into her reasons for forgoing her human shape, so I didn’t.”

Syl hissed at him.

Really, Syl? I shot at her. **You really think it’s a good idea to take on a vampire? What are you going to do, give him cat scratch fever?**

Fortunately, Alberto wasn’t offended by her attitude. “Your secret is safe with me, little one.” He considered her a moment, head tipped on one side. “Although I suspect your secret is out now, yes? Something feels different about you. Why did you take human form after all this time?”

“Someone forced her to,” I said.

“Who would do a thing like that?” Alberto slid onto the barstool next to me, as if he was ready to hear all my secrets.

Sadly for him, I wasn’t ready to tell them. “We have enemies.”

“A pretty girl like you?” He all but fluttered his eyelashes at me. They were thick and dark, too. Any girl would kill for eyelashes like that.

“Even pretty girls can make enemies,” I said primly.

He sighed, and dialled back the charm. “I wish you’d tell me who you really are. You can trust me.”

“There’s no secret about who I am.” Just what. “I’m Lexi Jardine.”

"Just an ordinary girl with powerful enemies?"

I wished I could tell him everything. He'd been nothing but a friend to me since we'd arrived, giving me a job at the bookstore, and what I was sure was reduced rent on the little apartment above it. He was like a kindly uncle, always watching out for me.

"I don't want to go into details," I said. "Trusting people hasn't worked out well for me in the past."

His eyes glittered strangely in the dim room. "You know I could kill you both without even exerting myself."

"I suppose you could." I kept my voice calm with an effort. Could he hear my heartbeat speed up?

He smiled, letting his fangs peep out. In three months this was only the second time I'd seen them.

Oh, crap, said Syl.

"Not that I would, of course." The fangs disappeared again and I allowed myself one deep, relieved breath. "A publican doesn't keep his customers long if people start disappearing from his establishment. I'm merely pointing out that if I'd wanted you dead, you would be. Perhaps a modicum of trust is in order?"

He got up and went behind the bar. I watched him get out two glasses and pour us both a shot of whisky. I felt a little more comfortable with the bar between us.

Did I trust him? More than I trusted most people, I guess.

"That's no way to live, you know." It was as if he could read my thoughts. "You have to trust someone, or you end up like a wild animal, cringing from every hand that reaches out to it." He eyed Syl, whose delicate pink tongue had darted out to lick up a couple of drops of amber fluid that had spilled onto the bar. "Or like a shifter who's too afraid to leave the shelter of her animal form."

I took a gulp of my drink, feeling the alcohol burn its way down my throat. I set it down with a clink, leaving a small ring on the gleaming wood surface of the bar, and came to a decision.

"A man called Erik Anders wanted me to find something for him. He's a shaper."

"The new councillor."

"Yes." I took another quick sip and set the glass down again, watching the interlocking wet circles formed on the dark wood. Circles within circles. "The thing he wanted belonged to another, more powerful shaper."

"Why did he ask *you* to find this item for him?" The vampire took a sip of his own drink, watching me over the rim of his glass. "Was it anything to do with how you found those boys the other night?"

The man was sharp. Did I have *any* secrets from him?

"I'm good at finding things," I said.

"So?" he prompted when I stopped there. "Why not just do it?"

"Even if I didn't get killed in the process, I doubted he would let me live afterwards. He wouldn't want to risk anyone discovering his part in the theft."

"Hmm. And I assume he's now succeeded in tracking you down?"

"That lion shifter you ran out of here was one of his men." I drained the glass. "Hence the need to say goodbye."

"You're running again? Why not do what he wants and get it over with? You're not without friends here, you know. He might find it a little harder than he imagines to do away with you."

He looked so fierce as he said this, I felt a rush of warmth that had nothing to do with the alcohol. It was good to feel that someone had my back. But I couldn't be responsible for dragging my friends into danger with me. Even Alberto, powerful as he was, was vulnerable to a fireshaper's flames. Joe and Holly stood no chance. I couldn't live with myself if anything happened to them because of me.

"Unfortunately, he has friends of his own," I said. "Jake Steele turning up here at precisely this time seems an awfully big coincidence. He says he's on council business, but he knows Anders—and the lion shifter, though he pretended he didn't. I'm afraid he's mixed up in it, too."

"I doubt that. There's no love lost between Steele and Anders. And he's telling the truth about the council business." He leaned over the bar and lowered his voice, though we were the only ones here. “Have you ever heard of shadow shapers?”

“No.”

Shapers only came in five flavours: earth, air, fire, water and metal. Most could manipulate more than one element, though there would be one that was their prime or dominant element. Some rare individuals could work with as many as four elements, but I’d never heard of anyone being able to work with *shadows*. What did that even mean?

“They’re shadows of the First Shapers, though I suppose you could say that all shapers are shadows of the First Shapers, since it was from them that shaping ability came originally.”

“The First Shapers are just a myth, though.” No one really knew where shapers had come from; they’d always been there. Just as some people had blue eyes, some had shaping abilities. People with blue eyes normally didn’t try to enslave the ones who didn’t, of course, which had been the problem with the shapers for all of recorded history.

Which was why we now had human cities and shaper cities. Separation seemed the best answer—at least, it had been working for the last hundred years or so. More or less.

The vampire shook his head in disbelief. “What do they teach you in those human cities?”

I’d never told him I’d come from Newport, the biggest human-controlled city in New Holland. Apparently that didn’t matter: he’d figured it out for himself.

“My dear, the First Shapers are as real as you and I.”

I eyed him suspiciously, not sure if he was pulling my leg. “The First Shapers—the gods—are real?” All the shapers kept shrines to their chosen gods. Statues to one god or another were all over shaper territory. Even tiny Berkley’s Bay had a statue of Poseidon keeping watch over the waterfront. But no one other than the shapers paid more than lip service to them. Maybe once belief in them had been widespread, but in these modern times belief in a bunch of quarrelsome deities seemed oddly quaint. “They’ve been awfully quiet for the last millennia or two, in that case.”

“I see you’re not a believer. Well, the shapers of the Ruby Council certainly are, and if someone were stealing your gods’ magic and creating a new kind of shaper with it—one with the same kind of powers as the gods, though in a lesser form—you might be as troubled as they are.”

This was all too much to take in at this hour of the morning, on top of the evening I’d just had. Not only was he saying that the gods were real, but that someone was killing them. How did you kill a god? Wasn’t the whole point of godhood that you were immortal? “Steele is hunting stolen magic? Or these shadow shapers? What does that have to do with me?”

“Nothing. That’s the point. He has far too much on his plate right now to be concerned with a runaway thief and a cat shifter. He came to consult me about some curious messages he has been receiving."

"Why? Did he think they were from you?" Not that I really cared. I was more interested in the messages Steele had been exchanging with Anders, and what they had said about a certain missing altarpiece. All this business about gods and magic and mysterious shadows was way above my pay grade, if it was even true. I mean, I trusted Alberto, but this was a lot to swallow. Sure, the shapers believed it, but that didn't mean I had to.

"He suspects they may be from a mutual friend of ours who disappeared in rather suspicious circumstances."

"Well, as long as he's not here to disappear *me*."

"I really don't think so. He could even be an ally for you against Anders. Don't be so quick to run away, Lexi. If they've found you once they can do it again, and next time you may not have friends around who can help you."

Friends? Syl snorted. **Didn't he just finish telling us we should trust him because he hasn't killed us yet? What sort of friend says something like that?**

She sounded disgruntled.

I thought you liked Alberto?

I like my blood where it is, thanks very much. Are you done with the goodbyes yet? Let's hit the road before Steele comes back and stirs up more trouble.

She was right. This goodbye had turned into a much

longer conversation than I'd planned. I got up to leave.

"Thank you for everything." Now it came to the actual goodbye, I felt awkward. You can't exactly hug a vampire, can you? That would bring your neck way closer to those fangs than any sensible person would risk.

"You know where I am if you need me," he said.

I nodded, then left him there in the darkened pub, swirling a melting ice cube around in the bottom of his glass while the shadows gathered around him. Outside in the cold night air again, we hurried across the road. The street door at the bottom of the stairs opened at a touch.

I thought you locked this? Syl asked.

"So did I."

An anxious feeling clenched in my stomach as I took the stairs to the landing, a feeling that yawned into a pit of horror at the sight of Joe and Holly's front door standing wide open.

"Holly?"

I hesitated in the doorway. No one answered, so I took a few steps inside. The presents from the baby shower were piled up on the dining table in a festive heap of pink and blue wrappings. A couple lay on the floor, as if they'd been swept aside in a struggle, their ribbons knocked askew. A bunch of helium balloons floated above them, pretty in soft pastel shades.

"Holly? Are you here?"

No one in the bedrooms, or the bathroom. The apartment was no bigger than ours; there was nowhere to hide.

Lexi. In here.

I rounded the kitchen bench and found Syl sniffing at a pool of liquid that spread across the tiled floor. In its centre lay the smashed remains of a coffee mug.

Syl looked up at me, her green eyes anxious. *_I think she left in a hurry._*

We were still standing there, staring at the smashed mug in horror, when a phone began to ring.

I scrabbled around on the dining table and found it half-hidden by the pile of presents, vibrating urgently against the pitted wooden surface of the table. It was Holly's. I recognised the diamanté-studded case.

Answer it, Syl urged.

I fumbled it to my ear. "Hello?"

"Lexi! Just the person I was hoping to speak to."

The speaker's voice had a jolly tone that was all wrong for the situation I found myself in.

"Who is this?"

"Have you forgotten me so soon? Really, I thought I'd made more of an impression. It's Erik. Erik Anders."

Syl's tail lashed from side to side. All this time, we'd

been hiding from this guy. And now he'd found us. This was bad. Really bad.

"What do you want?" Was it too much to hope he had nothing to do with Holly's disappearance? Yes, of course it was. We were standing in Holly's apartment, and he was calling us on Holly's own phone. But how did he know we'd be here? Was he watching us right now? A chill shuddered down my spine at the thought.

"My desires haven't changed. I want you to work for me."

"Mine haven't either. I'm not interested." I flung my senses out, searching every animal mind in the vicinity, hoping to find some trace of the man on the other end of the line.

"And yet I feel sure I can change your mind."

There was a sudden heavy breathing and a familiar voice came on the line. "Lexi?"

"Holly! Are you all right?"

Anders' smarmy tones filled my ear again. "The lady is perfectly comfortable. As long as you get that ring for me, she will stay that way."

This felt like being trapped in a bad thriller movie. I knew what the next line had to be. "And if I don't?"

"I really think you should," he said, almost gently. No threats. He didn't have to put it into words. He was an underpowered fireshaper with big ambitions. I already knew the depths to which he was prepared to sink to get what he wanted. If I didn't deliver, Holly would die. "And Lexi? Let's keep it between ourselves, hmm? If you bring anyone else into it, that could be bad news for our friend and her baby. Get the ring and wait for further instructions. Keep this phone with you."

He hung up without waiting for an answer. I guess he didn't need to. It was pretty obvious what my answer would be. What else could I do but obey?

Syl leapt up onto the table and plopped herself down right in front of me. Her green eyes stared at me, unblinking.

Time to cut and run, she said.

For a moment I thought I'd heard wrong. "Run?" I repeated stupidly.

We can't save her. The tip of Syl's tail twitched, betraying the agitation she was trying to hide. She might have saved herself the trouble—I could feel the turmoil of her emotions through our link anyway. Fear dominated, laced with anger, but there was also a healthy dose of … guilt?

"We have to try." It was my fault Holly was in danger. I'd led that bastard right to her.

Lexi, we* can't. *This guy doesn't play by the rules. You know that. Sure, if we don't bring him the ring, he kills her. But if we do bring it, he still kills her, and he kills us, too.

She leapt down from the table and headed for the door. **Whatever we do, she dies. There's no way to win this one. The best we can do is run, and hope that this time he doesn't find us.**

She didn't mention my break-in at Johnson's place, though I could feel the accusation lurking at the forefront of her mind. She thought that had led Anders to us. I was horribly afraid she was right. This was all my fault.

That just made me more determined to find a way out of this mess for all of us. I tucked Holly's phone into my back pocket and followed Syl across the landing into our own apartment.

"I'll think of something." I started piling things into a backpack: spare clothes, my throwing knives, a set of lock picks. I wished I still had my bow, but that was hardly a discreet weapon; I'd had to leave it behind when I'd left the human territories. I could cheerfully have used Anders for target practice right then. "I'm not abandoning Holly. She's my friend."

And there weren't too many people I could say that about.

I like her just as much as you do, Syl said, **but it's too late for her. All we can do is save ourselves.**

I frowned at her. "The old Syl wouldn't have said that. You've been a cat too long."

The old Syl hadn't watched her whole life go up in flames* *in front of her. Anders is a shaper. Your knives aren't going to do jack shit against him.

I zipped the pack shut. There was precious little in it. Most of our stuff had been left behind when we fled the city. Now we travelled lighter than light. Not much to show for a life, but possessions weren't that important when it came down to it. No one lay on their deathbed wishing they'd collected more *stuff*. People were what mattered.

"You can run if you want." I shouldered the backpack and looked down at the dainty black cat perched on the bed. *Still* she wouldn't take human form. When she'd showed herself to Holly earlier, I'd thought we'd had a breakthrough, but this latest development had obviously been too much for her. "But I'm going after Holly. Joe would hunt me down and kill me if I let anything happen to her."

Her tail twitched impatiently. **This is no time for jokes.**

"Who's joking? I reckon he would. Are you coming or not?"

And who could blame him? It wasn't just Holly's life at stake—there was the baby, too. It just showed what a lowlife scum Anders was, that he could threaten an innocent baby's life. Someone needed to do something about that guy.

And since I couldn't tell anyone what was going on, it looked like that someone would have to be me.

Shame I couldn't get a powerful shaper like Steele on my side. I bet he could put Anders in his place. But looking like he'd stepped off the cover of a romance novel didn't make Steele a hero—far from it. I couldn't trust him any more than I could trust Anders. In fact, they were probably working together. It was more than a little suspicious that Anders had found me right after Steele turned up, whatever Alberto said. Shapers were all the same. The sensible thing would be to rescue Holly and then disappear right out of Mr Hot Councillor's life.

And if sensible left a taste of disappointment in my mouth, well, I'd get over it. There'd be time to regret the loss of that perfect arse and chiselled jaw later, if I managed to live through whatever Anders had planned for me.

I hurried down the stairs with only a brief backward glance for the little apartment. I'd been happy, in spite of the horror that had led us here, and that paranoid feeling of being watched that had taken weeks to shrug off. Resentment boiled through me as I unlocked my beat-up old car and threw the pack into the back seat. Syl leapt into the passenger seat, pointedly not talking to me. Damn Anders and his schemes. When would he stop hounding us over this stupid ring? I'd have liked to take the thing and hurl it into the sea right next to the mayor's altarpiece.

How the hell was I going to get us all out of this alive?

I drove through the dark streets, my thoughts churning.

Holly's life and the baby's—all our lives—depended on a lot of things. Whether I was as good a burglar as Anders thought. Whether this damn ring was even still where he'd told me it was three months ago.

And whether a lone human with a slightly quirky ability could hope to outmanoeuvre a shaper with the power of fire at his command.

The sound of the engine split the night as I headed for the highway and Crosston, three hours' drive away.

It wasn't looking hopeful for the good guys.

12

The sun was struggling over the horizon by the time we hit the outskirts of Crosston. I'd lost track of how many times Holly's phone had rung on the trip. Each time, I'd checked the caller ID in case it was Anders again, but each time it had been Joe. The poor guy would be beside himself with worry, but I couldn't answer. Nothing good could come of dragging him into this mess. Werewolves were passionate creatures. No telling what he'd do if he heard his beloved wife had been kidnapped. Holly's safety depended on my silence, so I let the phone ring, feeling like the worst friend in the world.

Syl hadn't exactly been the most talkative travelling companion, but she'd clammed up completely about half an hour earlier, and now stared out the window, her green eyes expressionless. I stayed out of her head and gave her some room. Coming back was hard.

I stayed away from our old neighbourhood—the fewer people who knew we were in town the better—but even so there were reminders all around us. The bridge with its distinctive coat hanger shape, the Great Amphitheatre, the familiar streets sloping down to the harbour. Even I was affected, and I hadn't grown up here like Syl. Everywhere I looked, I saw reminders of the life we'd lived, until it seemed I could smell smoke on the air. I turned the air vents to recycle and blasted the aircon through the car.

Everywhere, too, was the shaper presence. Official buildings flying flags in the shaper colours of ruby, sapphire, emerald, gold and diamond, ice sculptures that defied both the heat and gravity in front of some watershaper's house, the twisted metal architecture that the fireshapers favoured for their office buildings. They liked to leave the visitor in no doubt. *This is our town*, shouted the buildings and the flags. *Shapers live here*, said the statues shooting flame, and the intricate ice carvings that never melted. *Like it or leave.*

I found a parking station and dumped the car. My rubber-soled shoes made no noise on the pavement as I made my way through quiet streets to Central Park, Syl cradled in my arms. It might look a little odd to be carrying a cat through the streets, but not as odd as having one follow at your heels like a dog, and neither of us wanted to split up. Office buildings loomed overhead, blocking the rising sun and making dark canyons of the streets below. I walked briskly, not meeting the eyes of the passers-by. They were mostly early birds turning up for work, though I passed a few joggers. None of them were shapers. The privileged classes didn't get up this early.

I chose a quiet spot away from the main paths and sat down on the grass, which was still a little damp with morning dew. Syl disappeared into the bushes on her own errands—or maybe she just wanted to get away from me. Our mental link bristled with resentment and fear, and she hadn't spoken a word. Office buildings encircled the park, their shadows stretching over the grass, except to the east. Shading my eyes, I squinted into the sun and stared at the long, low building there, its towers just clearing the tops of the trees. The Ruby Palace.

It was the most famous building in the city, and the most heavily guarded—the home of the Ruby Adept, leader of the fireshapers in New Holland and head of the Ruby Council.

It was also the place I had to break into. No pressure.

Hugging my knees to me, I closed my eyes and reached out with my mind. Not surprisingly, there were quite a few animals in range. The park was a vast green space in the centre of the city and though there were plenty of manicured picnic lawns, there were also wild spaces scattered throughout it. Lots of cats and dogs roamed the city streets, but a handful of foxes called the park home, and a colony of bats lit up like a Christmas tree to my mental vision as they climbed over each other and jostled for the best spots to sleep the day away. There were rodents and birds everywhere, plus fish in the ornamental lakes. Working with fish was hard. I connected best with warm-blooded creatures, though I could link with anything in a pinch, even reptiles or insects.

I skipped over the bright sparks of life outside, however. Later, I would use the birds to check the exterior views, but right now I was concerned with the inside of one building in particular.

Thankfully there were nearly always mice in a building that size, and this early in the day it was safe to send them scuttling about the interior. I lay back on the grass at the foot of a massive fig tree and shut my eyes, the better to focus on the guided tour.

The Ruby Palace had only three levels, but what it lacked in height it made up for in sprawl. Just as well there was more than one mouse, because the place covered a whole city block, and the ground floor was a maze of rooms, large and small. The main audience hall was a vast, echoing emptiness at the heart of the building, surrounded by corridors that snaked like veins through the rest of it. It looked like what it was: a building that had been added to several times over the years, resulting in a confusion of passageways and hidden nooks that nearly did my head in trying to keep straight.

The morning heated up as I lay there, searching the palace through beady mouse eyes. I was pretty sure I wouldn't find the ring on the ground floor, but I still wanted to have the layout committed to memory. Life had taught me always to expect the unexpected. There was no telling where I might have to run, or who might be chasing me at the time.

I wished I'd never heard of this damned ring—it had brought me nothing but trouble. I still had no idea how I was going to save Holly. All the advantages lay with Anders, and I couldn't see a way to turn the situation to my advantage. Fear lay like a heavy weight on my chest. I had to force myself to focus on what I was doing. The first step was to get the ring; I'd worry about the rest of it later.

I flung a hand over my eyes; though they were closed, the sun made bright orange patterns on the inside of my lids as the shade from the branches overhead moved. My skin prickled with heat and my stomach gurgled a protest at the lack of food—hours had passed, and I'd missed breakfast. When I reached out through our link to Syl I found she was doing what cats do best: she was curled up in the sun somewhere asleep.

A shadow fell across my face. I opened my eyes and shot upright, pulse racing. Steele stood over me, his face stern and unreadable as he gazed down at me. "Where's Holly?" he asked.

"I don't know." How had he found me? And why was he looking at me like that?

His eyes were as icy as a winter storm. "Bullshit." He grabbed my arm and jerked me to my feet. "You've got her phone. Where is she?"

I tried to tug my arm free, but his grip was as hard as the look on his face. I started to deny it, but he frisked me one-handed and pulled Holly's phone from my back pocket. If possible, his look was even grimmer as he dangled it in front of my eyes.

"Joe will be tearing Berkley's Bay apart by now, looking for her. When I dropped him home and he found the place abandoned and both of you gone, he assumed the baby was on the way and you must have taken Holly to hospital. I'm afraid I wasn't so trusting." The way he was looking at me, you'd have thought I was something stinky he'd scraped off the bottom of his shoe. My own temper began to rise. Exactly what was he accusing me of? "He went off to the hospital, expecting to find his wife in labour. I, on the other hand, had her phone traced, and followed it all the way to the city."

"And what were you expecting to find? That Holly and I had run off together? Or that I'd killed her?" I finally succeeded in shaking off his hand, and glared at him, putting my own on my hips. "What kind of person do you think I am? Holly and Joe are my friends. I wouldn't do anything to hurt them. Not that I expect a *shaper* to grasp the concept of friendship."

He folded his arms, though I was in no mood to admire the strong muscles of his forearms now. Though for just a moment there, when I'd first opened my eyes and seen him, his face had been the best thing I'd seen all day.

"Enlighten me, then. Explain what's going on."

The ice in the depths of his blue eyes had melted, and a fire now danced there instead. It occurred to me that enraging a fireshaper with cheap shots may not have been the smartest thing to do. I lifted my chin and held his burning gaze, but said nothing. Holly's safety depended on my not telling anyone what was going on. He could go douse himself in the lake if he expected me to lose the chance to save her.

He growled in frustration and stepped in close, gripping my shoulders. "If there is a more infuriating woman in the world, Apollo *forbid* I ever meet her. Talk to me, Lexi. If you don't, you can tell it to the provosts instead." His fingers tightened. "Was that a flinch? You don't like that idea?"

Of course I didn't like that idea. Who would? The provosts were the shapers' police force. Most of them weren't shapers themselves, but they'd taken on their masters' view of the world, and their reputation for bastardry was enough to make even the most innocent citizens avoid them. No one in their right mind would want to be taken in by the provosts. And if I were arrested now, before I could steal the ring and swap it for Holly, what would happen to her?

Shit. I stared up at that handsome face, so close to my own, and all I wanted to do was punch it. Why did bloody Jake Steele have to get involved? I'd had this under control. More or less.

"What's it going to be, Lexi? I'm not a patient man."

Oh, really? *His* patience was running out? Why did he always seem to be turning up lately, getting in my face? He could ruin everything. I stared at him in silent defiance.

"I can make you tell me. Do you need another demonstration?" Flames burst from his hands and licked up his arms.

I knocked his hands away, burning myself in his fire. "Will you cut that out?" I hissed. One of my wrists was badly scorched and throbbed with agony. "Don't make a scene here, right in front of the damn Palace."

The park would be swarming with guards and provosts in a heartbeat, and there would go my last hope of saving Holly. I cast a quick, fearful glance around. A young couple hurried away, clearly deciding this wasn't a safe place for their morning tea after all. No one else had noticed his display yet.

He caught my arms in strong, though thankfully no longer burning, hands. "Give me one good reason why I shouldn't."

I couldn't see any way out. If he got Holly killed with his arrogant demands, I would never forgive him.

"Holly's been kidnapped," I admitted, my voice full of the resentment that seethed beneath my skin. "And I'm the only one who can save her."

His face was a mask, but I could tell by the way he shifted that I'd surprised him. "Kidnapped? By whom?"

"Your mate, Erik Anders."

His focus intensified. "And what's your involvement?"

"*My* involvement? I should be asking *you* that question. Are you working with Anders?"

"Anders is a fellow councillor. That's the extent of our connection." That was what Alberto had said, too, but I wasn't convinced.

I threw my hands up in disgust, shrugging out of his grasp. "See? That's the whole problem with you. You've done nothing but accuse me of lying since we met, when you're lying through your teeth yourself. You expect me to believe Anders' little errand boy Mason just happened to turn up right after *you* showed up in town? You even lied about knowing him!"

He ignored my questions. "Why are you the only one who can save her?"

But now that I was in rant mode, it all came tumbling out. "I don't even know why you dislike me so much. What terrible crime do you suspect me of? I've never done anything to earn this amount of suspicion. Do you think I'm a One Worlder? Is that it?"

"I think you may be something infinitely worse."

"There's something worse than One Worlders? I thought you shapers hated them all with the fire of a thousand suns." A small sun burned on my wrist where he'd scorched me. I was too scared to look at the damage. Then I remembered what else Alberto had said, just before I left, about Steele's reason for visiting him. "You think I'm a shadow shaper, don't you?"

He went so still that I knew I'd hit the jackpot.

"What do you know about shadow shapers?" His voice was silk over steel, filled with menace.

I took a step back. "Only what Alberto told me. That you were worried about them, and that you'd been getting cryptic messages from a friend that they'd taken."

"Alberto must really trust you, to pass on my confidences so lightly." He let out a deep breath, and his hostility seemed to go with it. He took my hand, gently this time, and turned it over to look at the bright red marks of his fingers on my wrist. "I hurt you. I'm sorry."

Did that mean he'd decided to trust me because Alberto did? Once again my vampire friend was coming to my rescue, though he wasn't even here.

I wasn't quite as ready to let go of my anger. Steele's apology didn't stop my wrist stinging like the devil, and I was determined to get to the bottom of his connection with my enemy.

"Did you tell Anders you found me, like a good little lapdog?"

His expression turned to one of revulsion. "I am *not* Anders' lapdog. And why would I tell him anything about you? I don't tell the councillors about every girl who tries to kiss me, you know."

"Not *that.*" I could feel my face heating. "You emailed him about the break-in at the Mayor's house. I saw the email on your laptop."

He frowned. "That was *you*?"

Way to incriminate yourself, Lexi. Syl chose that moment to saunter out of the trees and pin me with a look of disgust.

Oops.

"So much for Johnson's gang of cat shifters. I emailed the whole council with my report—which was basically that Johnson is full of shit—and Anders emailed back. He was very interested in the details." He glanced at Syl. "He particularly wanted to know if a black cat was involved."

Just as I'd feared. That break-in had been what tipped Anders off to our presence. "And then he sent Mason," I said.

"It seems so. Now go back to the part where you tell me what you have to do with the reason Anders has kidnapped Holly—if that's really what's happened."

"Trust me, that's what's happened. Although I suppose it was Mason that did the actual kidnapping, while you and Joe were out looking for him. Anders wants her for leverage over me. He wants me to do something for him, and he figured threatening my friend would force me into it."

And he was right, the bastard.

The confusion began to clear from Steele's face. "This thing he wants you to do, does it involve breaking into the Ruby Palace?"

I drew in a sharp breath. "How did you know that?"

His face lit with grim satisfaction. "I *knew* he was working with the shadow shapers. Go on. Tell me everything."

Ha. Not likely. But I told him enough to keep him happy: about the ring, and Anders' previous attempt to get me to steal it. How Syl and I had fled town, but Anders had found us again. His expression grew darker as I talked.

"So," I said, "any idea why your new councillor wants to steal a ring from the Ruby Adept's safe? What's so special about this ring, anyway?"

"Let's just say it would be very bad for the fireshapers if Anders got his hands on it. If the *shadow shapers* got their hands on it."

"Don't suppose you want to help me get in there and get it, do you?" The place was riddled with security cameras. It wouldn't be impossible, but walking in as the guest of one of the councillors would certainly be easier than going it alone.

"You're asking the wrong guy. I've suspected for a while that Anders had bigger plans than just making it onto the council. But the Ruby Adept won't hear a word against his favourite, and I'm seriously out of favour at the moment." A wry grin momentarily turned his grim countenance into something far more attractive. "The Adept seized on Johnson's complaints about his town being overrun by rampaging cat shifters. Left me in no doubt that I needed to spend more time in my role as Master of the South-East, and that I wouldn't be required to return to the capital for quite some time. However …" The grin turned malicious. "I have floorplans of the Palace I can show you."

"So you're not going to try to stop me stealing the ring?"

"No. I'll help you free Holly. I owe Joe that much. If I hadn't dragged him out of his bed, he would have been there to protect Holly himself."

Right. As if Joe could have done anything that Holly herself couldn't. Being pregnant didn't make her any less a werewolf. But I was willing to let that point slide, if it meant Steele would help me against Anders. Having a fireshaper up my sleeve would be an ace in the hole against whatever betrayal Anders had planned—because he definitely had a double-cross planned. There was no way he could afford to let me walk out of there with Holly, knowing what I knew.

"And after I get the ring?"

"I'll make a copy of it for you to give to Anders."

"Really?" Now it was my turn to sound doubtful. "An exact copy? Anders said it had some fancy sunburst design on it."

"Not a problem. My secondary is metalshaping."

I'd figured as much after seeing him make those handcuffs out of the barstool leg. Most fireshapers' secondary element was either metal or earth. At least if it came to a fight, Steele should prove stronger than Anders, whose secondary was water.

Syl sniggered. *_Oh, that's rich._*

What?

His name's Steele and he's a metalshaper? You should ask him if that's his real name or a stage name.

Very funny.

"I'll keep the original safe," Steele continued. At least someone was focused on the job. I threw Syl a withering look but she licked one dainty paw, airily ignoring me. "You can trade the copy for Holly, then I'll burst in with the provosts and catch him red-handed with the ring. Then I'll have proof for the Ruby Adept that his favourite is crooked."

"Why bother making a copy, then? If it all goes to plan, Anders will only have it for a few moments." It seemed a lot of effort to go to. The more I heard about this ring, the more curious I became. What was the big deal with it?

He pulled a face. "Because the gods laugh at the plans of men."

13

"He'll probably be working late tonight," said Steele. We were in the sleek red sports car again, though the roof was up this time, enclosing us in an intimate, dark space. "There's a special council meeting tomorrow, so he'll be in his office on the lower floor. There shouldn't be anyone in his private rooms."

The car was parked in a dark spot a couple of streets from the Ruby Palace. The streetlights illuminated Steele's strong profile next to me. The sooner I got out of this car the better. I needed to be concentrating on the job, not distracted by thoughts of how good he looked in the dim light, or how close his powerful body was.

But then, anyone looked good if it was dark enough. Just because he'd spent the afternoon going over floorplans and photos of the Palace with me, and talking about the routines of the guards, there was no need to go weak at the knees. He'd applied a cooling ointment to my burns and bandaged my arm almost tenderly—but he was the one who'd caused the damage in the first place. I had to remember he was a shaper, not one of the good guys.

"I thought the council only met once a month."

"So they do, unless something important comes up." I gathered it was something to do with the mysterious shadow shapers. He didn't seem inclined to elaborate. Perhaps he thought Alberto had told me too much already. "Anders is just the tip of the iceberg."

Several times during the afternoon, I'd caught him staring intently at me. What did he see that was so interesting? Was he still secretly worried that I was in league with his enemies? But it wasn't that kind of a look. It was more intrigued than wary.

The mice had found the safe for me, hidden behind a painting in the Ruby Adept's private apartments. Not the most original hiding place, but what it lacked in originality it made up for in inaccessibility. Even Steele, a member of the council, had never been inside his boss's private apartments. Apparently no one was allowed in, apart from the Adept himself, a handful of guards, and his trusted personal servants.

Not that that would matter to me. I'd already worked out my plan of attack, and I was confident I could do this.

Steele didn't seem to share my confidence. "I'll try to get you out if you get caught."

"Thanks," I said drily. "Let's hope that won't be necessary."

Holly was depending on me. Getting caught wasn't an option. I put my hand on the door handle. Time to go.

"Wait." Steele leaned toward me. Before I realised what he was doing, he had my face cupped in both hands. "For luck."

His lips descended on mine, soft and hard at the same time. I froze in surprise, then heat jolted through me, and suddenly I was kissing him back, my fingers reaching up to twine through his hair and pull him even closer. What was I doing? This guy was a shaper, one of the enemy. But holy shit, he could kiss. Everywhere he touched, my senses burst into flame, and I melted against him, kissing him back hungrily.

How long had it been since anyone had touched me like this? For a second I forgot what I was doing—forgot Holly, forgot the ring and the danger awaiting me, forgot everything but Steele's mouth searing its way into my being, his hands roaming over my body, lighting new fires wherever they touched.

When we broke apart, we were both breathing heavily.

The intensity of his expression made me nervous, so I blurted out the first smart comment that came into my head. "Are all fireshapers so … changeable? This morning you were threatening to turn me over to the provosts for questioning."

"You didn't really think I'd do that, did you?" His knuckles grazed lightly along my jawline, sending a thrill of delight shooting through my body. "I had to say something to get you to talk. You are the most stubborn woman I've ever met."

He continued to stroke my face, his eyes focused on my lips. This was *not* conducive to my concentration. Shakily I reached for the door before my insides exploded and I melted into his arms. Even reminding myself that he was a shaper couldn't stop my knees from trembling.

I practically fell onto the pavement. "See you later."

"I'll be waiting." His deep voice was full of promise.

Infuriating man. I slammed the door and turned away, taking deep breaths of the cool night air. What was he thinking, kissing me like that? Where did he get the idea that I would welcome that kind of attention?

I don't know. Probably from the way you tried to climb into his lap like you were a starving kitten and he was a big bowl of milk.

Oh, great. I'd been hoping Syl hadn't seen that.

It's not polite to intrude on people's private moments.

**You were in a car in the middle of a public street. You need to work on your definition of* private.*

A small black cat stalked out of an alley and fell into step beside me as I passed, her tail waving haughtily in the air. Thankfully, she didn't say anything further about my questionable behaviour. She could hardly have said anything I wasn't already saying to myself.

As we approached the palace I pushed all further thoughts of Steele out of my head. I couldn't afford the distraction. I opened my mind to the life all around me, which helped me leave thoughts of the self behind. The world was bigger than just me and my issues. I touched a hundred little lives, all busy with their own affairs: here an owl out hunting, there a mouse skittering through the undergrowth in the park, further off a dog baying at the moon. I reaffirmed my link to the bright spark that was Syl, and joined with a couple of other cats, too. Their agility would serve me well.

We arrived at the street that ran along the back of the palace. A neat garden lay on the other side of the high iron fence. The fireshapers' taste ran to traditional rose beds with pebbled paths meandering between them, and the heady scent of the blooms hung on the night air.

Wait here, I told Syl. My plan called for smaller allies tonight.

I walked along the pavement beside the fence, just another woman hurrying home in the night. The palace grounds were softly lit, but as Steele had predicted, the top floor of windows were dark. Most of the lights were on the second floor, where the offices were, and a couple more on the ground floor. My mental map of the building suggested that was the security centre.

There were cameras on the high fences and up under the eaves of the building. Cameras everywhere, their eyes unblinking. I sent out a call and first one, then another, answered. Small bodies flapped and crawled—it only needed one or two. A cockroach covered the camera lens on top of the fence long enough to hide my leap to the top and quick drop on the other side. Another obligingly settled on the rooftop camera covering that section of the grounds. Only for a moment—not long enough to arouse suspicion, but long enough to hide my quick dash across the open lawn.

Pressed against the side of the building, I waited to see if the alarm would be raised, but nothing disturbed the still night. It was after midnight. There was no one else on the street. I wondered what time the Ruby Adept would start thinking longingly of his pillow. I'd have thought of mine, except then I might think about sharing it with a certain fire-eyed shaper, and that would be no good for either my blood pressure or my concentration.

The cameras were angled to cover the grounds, not the sides of the building, which was made of the local sandstone. Plenty of cracks and little bumps and ledges to make the ascent easy for a cat-like climber. I took advantage and climbed rapidly.

From the roof, I had a view of the night-time city. The main thoroughfares were lit with streetlamps, but great swathes of the city bulked in darkness. Guess the shapers didn't think it worthwhile to light the way for mere humans or shifters in those poorer neighbourhoods.

Skyscrapers were out of fashion—they were seen as too "human". Even the tallest buildings were only four or five storeys high. None sprawled across as much ground as the complex on whose roof I lay.

Again, I waited to see if I'd triggered any alarms, but nothing stirred to break the silence of the wee hours. There was a guard on the third-floor balcony below me. He was stationed outside the apartments of the Ruby Adept. Another guard stood in the interior corridor outside the Adept's door, according to my little spies. I wondered if they stood there all night. Must be the most boring guard duty ever. The poor bastard on the balcony couldn't even pace, since the balcony was neither wide nor long.

I gathered my forces again, ready for the final assault. Poor man. I felt guilty as I crept across the roof to a position just above his head.

The cockroaches swarmed, and muffled swearing broke the stillness of the night, followed by the sound of a man slapping himself in some agitation. I risked a peek. The poor man was doing well not to scream. He must have had fifty cockroaches crawling on him, and half of them were on his face. I shuddered even as I leapt off the roof.

My kick caught him in the head and he went down like

a sack of potatoes. A handful of my little soldiers crunched underneath him, the small sparks of their lives blinking out in my mind. Hurriedly I let the others go. They flitted and scurried away, leaving me alone on the balcony with the guard.

I checked his pulse. It beat strongly, but he was out cold. Quickly I gagged him with the handkerchief from his pocket and tied him up with his own belt, in case he woke before I was finished. Then I turned to the balcony door and stepped inside, pulling it closed behind me.

I was in a lounge room, furnished predominantly in red. Looked like the Ruby Adept took his title seriously. A single lamp by the door—red, of course—lent a bloody glow to the scene. Either the Adept was a neat man or his servants were very particular; it looked like a hotel room awaiting a guest. Nothing out of place, no sign that anyone lived here. There wasn't even a newspaper on the coffee table, much less any personal possessions.

Moving quietly, I crossed to the inner door. Through here was a bedroom, a bathroom, and an enormous walk-in wardrobe. It was nearly as big as the bedroom. How many clothes did one man need? A lot, apparently. One whole wall was nothing but suits. Another was devoted to his official robes of office—red, naturally.

The bedroom looked more like someone's actual home. Two cats were curled in the middle of the large bed. One raised its head to look at me dispassionately. The other didn't even stir. Opposite the bed hung a life-sized portrait of the Adept, looking entirely too pleased with himself. Did he ever have any lady friends here? And if so, what did they think of having that supercilious face smirking down at them all night?

The room was neat: a set of brushes on the dressing table, a book on the table by the bed with a pair of glasses folded neatly on top. There was also a small shrine to Apollo, heavy with gold, with a much smaller painting of the god above it. Apollo might not be too impressed that his painting was barely a quarter the size of the one of his worshipper, but I was relieved. That was the one that hid the safe. It would be a hell of a lot easier to get off the wall than the other monstrosity.

Some people had the bright idea of attaching their paintings to the wall in such a way that they could swing easily to reveal the safe behind them. I didn't approve of such arrangements; hinges made it all too obvious that a painting was meant to be moved, and therefore that it hid something of value. The Ruby Adept was obviously of my school of thought, because Apollo's painting hung from a simple hook. After checking for traps, I lifted it free and leaned it against the wall. The more alert of the cats wandered over to see what I was doing, while its fellow snoozed on.

Now came the interesting part. I wasn't much of a safe-cracker. Most of the time I didn't need to be. People had a terrible tendency to leave combinations written in obvious places, because they were afraid of forgetting them, or using sequences of numbers, like birthdates, that were relatively simple to predict. That was if they even bothered with safes at all. Far more often I would find whatever valuable I sought hidden in a sock drawer, or underneath the mattress.

Steele had assured me, however, that the Ruby Adept did use his safe. And no, Steele didn't know the combination. That would have been too easy. What he had given me instead was a little gizmo of his own invention. All I had to do, apparently, was attach it to the safe, flick the switch and stand well clear.

Oh, and hope like hell that the noise didn't bring the guards running. Steele had been a little evasive on that point.

I weighed the little thing in my hand, letting my mind wander out into the building. Further into the palace, a mouse climbed inside the walls. Several cockroaches lurked in the dark places behind the furniture and a large spider clung to the wall high up around a bend in the corridor, waiting for an unwary insect. Apart from the cats in the room with me, nothing else stirred on this floor …

Wait. The spider's vision showed me a figure hurrying

past. Was it the Ruby Adept? It was hard to tell, but it seemed likely. Who else would be awake at this time of night?

Shit shit shit. I lifted the painting of Apollo, flinching as it bumped against the wall, and tried to rehang it. In my haste I missed the hook the first time. I swallowed hard, forcing myself to slow down enough to do it properly. As I got it hung, I heard voices in the hallway outside the apartment. Hell. Where would I hide?

I scurried into the walk-in wardrobe and pushed in among the scarlet robes as the latch clicked. Not the greatest hiding spot, and if the Ruby Adept was in the mood to examine his wardrobe with any great care, I'd be discovered. His cat looked enquiringly at me from the bedroom door, and I gave it a quick mental shove. Obligingly it leapt back onto the bed and settled down, resting its chin on the other cat. I tried to slow my breathing, wishing I could join my mouse friend inside the safety of the walls.

From here I could see into the bedroom, and the doorway of the bathroom. The damn Apollo painting hung a little crooked. That was bad, but it was too late to do anything about it. Soft footfalls crossed the carpet, and a red-clothed back disappeared into the bedroom.

I held my breath. Would he notice the painting hanging askew?

I heard a yawn, and then two soft thunks—probably shoes hitting the floor. He murmured endearments to the cats, and then the bedsprings creaked. Oh, no. *Please don't go to bed yet.* I'd have to wait for him to fall asleep before I dared attempt the safe again. And surely he wouldn't sleep through Steele's little explosion? Would I have to knock out the Ruby Adept himself? He was the most powerful fireshaper in the country. And there was that guard out on the balcony. How long before he woke up? This was all going to shit.

I forced a deep breath, and then another. Panic wasn't going to help. I'd been in tight situations before—I could find a way out of this one.

The Ruby Adept sauntered back into my view, now stark naked. He was a large man with a hairy chest. Thankfully, he didn't head my way. He paused in the doorway to the bathroom to scratch absently under one armpit, allowing me a view of a back every bit as hairy as his front, then disappeared into the bathroom. A moment later, I heard the shower start.

I drew a shuddery breath of relief and stepped out of my hiding place. Now I had just one problem. In addition to his sagging, hairy nakedness, the Adept's pause in the doorway had shown me one other thing:

The ring on his little finger in the shape of a stylised sun.

14

Okay, so there was good news and bad news. The good news was that I didn't have to blow the safe. The bad news was that somehow I had to get the ring off the Ruby Adept's finger without him seeing me. He was the most powerful fireshaper in the country; giving him a chance at a shot at me would be fatal. Even if I did somehow manage to survive and escape, no way did I want my face appearing on Wanted posters, and him with a personal vendetta against me.

Likewise, I suspected Steele would be really peeved with me if I managed to kill the head of his Council, accidently or otherwise. What was a girl to do in a tight situation?

The more alert cat regarded me from the bedroom doorway, probably wondering if I was going to banish it again. I called it to me, and it wound itself affectionately around my legs. I bent down to stroke its sleek head, the glimmerings of a plan forming in my head.

The clock was against me here. Any time now, that guard on the balcony could wake up. Probably the first thing he would do was start kicking the wall—or some other noisy, attention-grabbing thing. I had to be gone before then.

The noise of running water shut off. The Adept was a quick showerer. Score one for me. I stepped to the side of the bathroom door and flattened myself against the wall, drawing a knife from its sheath. Not that I was planning on sticking the Adept with it—I was a burglar, not a murderer. Unlike the shapers.

I called the sleepy cat from the bedroom and it came to join us, though I earned a filthy look for disturbing it. I held them both there, ready to implement my flimsy plan.

The Ruby Adept was towelling himself dry, singing in an off-key drone. I heard the squeak of a towel rail as he hung the towel back up, then his heavy tread approaching the door. The cats sprang into action.

"Hello, my beauties. Yes, yes, I love you too."

I set the cats to winding around his legs as he walked. One caught at his heel with her claws, while the other planted herself in the perfect spot to catch his other foot as he stepped away.

He landed heavily on his hands and knees on the carpet at my feet. He barely had time to register my boots standing so close to his face before I belted him on the back of the head with the hilt of my knife. He collapsed the rest of the way to the floor and lay still in all his naked, hairy glory.

Crouching at his side, I tugged the ring off his damp, fleshy finger. It was a golden sun, with twelve rays swirling out from the sun's face, and felt warm to the touch. Probably from the shower. I turned it over, but there was nothing engraved inside the band.

Something about it tugged at my memory. Had I seen it before somewhere? The sun was Apollo's symbol, of course, and it wasn't unusual to find it here in this shaper city. And there were only so many ways you could depict a sun. Nevertheless, the feeling that I'd seen this particular ring before persisted.

Sized for the Ruby Adept's large hands, it would be way too big for mine, yet I found myself sliding it onto the ring finger of my left hand. And it fit.

Something whispered on the edges of my hearing, and I whipped my head around. The cats and I were alone with the Adept's unconscious body. I strained my hearing to thc limits. The whisper came again, as indistinguishable as a conversation overhead in a distant room, and I realised the sound was within my head. It was coming from the ring.

I might have knelt there, staring at the ring glittering on my finger until the Adept awoke and incinerated me, except that his cat, tired of being ignored, butted me impatiently with her head.

"You did well, little one." I rubbed her sleek ears, strangely unperturbed by the magic that had shrunk the ring to fit, or even the odd, faint whispering. Shaper magic? I didn't care. It felt right, to have this ring on my finger. Familiar. Like coming home.

Home. That was a joke. I'd been chased out of my home, driven away for my "uncanny abilities". My brother murdered, my mother suspected of being a witch. I had no home any more.

I glanced at the ring. Its colour reminded me of my brother's golden hair, the way it had shone in the sun.

I flinched, tried to turn away from that memory, because it always led me to that final image of the blood matted in that shining hair as they carried his body away. I leapt up, startling the cat, and strode toward the balcony door, as if by moving I could leave the memory behind. That was all in the past anyway. Why continue to torture myself with memories of what I'd lost?

I eased open the door to the balcony. The guard was starting to stir, so I leapt lightly onto the balcony rail and pulled myself up onto the roof. The ring glinted in the moonlight.

Well, that would never do. I pulled it off my finger, though it almost pained me to hide its light, and shoved it deep into the front pocket of my pants, where I could feel it lodged against my hip bone.

I hurried across the roof to the point where I'd climbed up, my steps sure on the tiles. All I had to do was repeat the procedure in reverse. But faster. Any minute now that guard would raise the alarm and the gardens would be flooded with light and people. No amount of cockroaches could hide me then.

I inched my way back down the side of the building, my movements sure, though my mind was elsewhere. Why did Anders want this ring? What wasn't Steele telling me about it? It was clearly a ring of some power, and more power in the hands of a snake like Anders could never be a good thing. Steele meant to foil Anders' attempts to get his hands on it, but plans could go awry.

And if it all did go to plan, and the ring was returned to the Ruby Adept's fat finger? I was sure, as sure as I knew my own name, that the ring didn't belong there. The strength of that conviction was driving me nuts, because I didn't have a single damn fact to back it up. I just *knew*. Its presence in my mind, gone now that I no longer wore it, had felt eerily similar to my link to Syl, as if the ring were an old friend.

I reached the ground and stood there a moment, my face pressed against the rough sandstone, racking my brain. Where had I seen this ring before?

My hand resting lightly on the lump in my pocket, I summoned the cockroaches to mask the camera lenses before I made my run across the garden to the outer wall. I owed the shapers nothing, and trusting them to use this kind of power wisely was madness. My gut told me this ring was important.

Despite all Steele's care, the ring might disappear just as mysteriously as it had arrived.

Steele was waiting for me, parked around the first corner. Behind me, a shrill alarm began to sound. The guards would be scurrying in a panic. The Ruby Adept was down, bashed and robbed. This was no place to linger, yet I felt a great reluctance to get into that sleek red car.

What's the hold-up? Syl sounded impatient. Her green eyes glinted in the light from the streetlamps as she looked out the window at me. **Let's get out of here before someone arrests you.**

All I had to do was get into the car, and Steele would whisk me away to safety. The ring burned in my pocket like a live coal, its existence clouding my thoughts. I could keep walking. I knew how to disappear in the city. And Steele was a shaper. Since when had I trusted one of them? Why was Syl even sitting in his car, so relaxed? She hated shapers as much as I did.

My hand crept to my pocket, as if to assure myself it was really still there. Could I truly let him take it? The shapers had no right to it.

The car door swung open. Steele leaned across from the driver's seat. "Get in. We don't have much time."

Still I hesitated, the urge to run making my legs twitch. I'd go home. My mother would know. She'd always refused to discuss my ability to link to animals, but I was certain she knew where it had come from. She could tell me why this ring felt to my mind like a sleeping animal, one that I could link with if only I knew how to wake it.

What are you waiting for? A bloody gilt-edged invitation? Get your butt in here before this place is crawling with provosts.

I got in and shut the door.

Steele immediately pulled out and did a U-turn. "How did it go? Did you get it?"

"Yes."

His expression changed, alerted perhaps by the tone of my voice. "Any problems?"

I looked out the window at the dark streets sliding past. He was driving fast, but not so fast as to draw unwanted attention. "Not unless you call bashing the Ruby Adept over the head a problem."

He winced. "That's … unfortunate. Did he see your face?"

"No."

"Well, that's something, at least. What happened? Did he walk in on you cracking the safe?"

I leaned back in the seat and stroked the soft fur of Syl's ears. Sometimes it was hard to remember she'd ever been human. "I didn't have to crack anything." Except the Adept's head. "He was wearing it."

Steele gave me a sharp glance. "He was *wearing* it?"

"Is that a problem?"

"Yes. No." His teeth worried at his bottom lip. The effect was surprisingly erotic. I had to look away. "Maybe. We agreed to keep it locked up. It's not just any old ring."

"What kind of ring is it, then?"

I held my breath, waiting for the answer, but he just shook his head. "No issues with the cameras?"

Fine. He wanted to keep his super-secret shaper business to himself? I had other ways of finding out. "Nope."

"No wonder Erik wanted you. I would never have believed what you've just done was possible. Still not giving your professional secrets away?"

"Seems like we both have professional secrets."

My tone was a little sharp, maybe. Syl's voice sounded in my head. **You expect him to tell you all the secrets of the shapers? He's a councillor, you know. This shit is probably classified.**

Since when have you been an apologist for the shapers?

Since he started working against that bastard Anders.

Oh? The enemy of my enemy is my friend?

Not a friend, exactly, though he does give very nice belly* *rubs. You should ask him to give you one sometime. It might make you less grouchy.

Right. That would be the day.

Holly's phone, sitting in the console between us, began to ring. I snatched it up.

"Yes?" I put it on loudspeaker so Steele could hear.

"You have the ring?"

"Yes."

"Good. Meet me at the docks in fifteen minutes. There's a warehouse—"

"Stop right there," I said. Steele raised an eyebrow, but I ignored him. "I'm not bringing it anywhere at"—I checked my watch—"two-fifteen in the morning."

The voice on the other end of the line grew chilly. It wasn't Anders; it might have been Mason the lion guy, but I wasn't sure. "You're not in any position to be making demands. Do as you're told, if you want your werewolf friend back."

"See, that's the problem," I said, settling back more comfortably in my seat.

What the hell are you doing? Syl hissed, her claws digging into my leg through my jeans.

"I want Holly back safely; of course I do. But I'm not prepared to commit suicide for her. If I turn up at your nice abandoned warehouse in the middle of the night, you're just going to take the ring and kill us both. You've got to throw me a bone here."

"I don't have to throw you anything," he said, though he sounded less certain than before. "This is not a negotiation. You now have fourteen minutes."

"If I don't come, your boss doesn't get his ring."

"If you don't come, your friend and her baby never make it home."

"And then neither of us would be happy, right? So why don't you make it easy on yourself. Tell your boss I'll meet him somewhere public, in daylight. His choice."

And then I hung up.

Syl stared up at me, her eyes round. **You've got some big balls.**

Thanks. Now could you get your claws out of my leg?

Oh, sorry. That was a little nervewracking.

Yeah, for me too. I was sweating all over.

"Well done," Steele said. "That gives me some time to organise back-up."

"You have to be careful," I said. "You can't let Anders know what you're doing. If he finds out I've told someone …"

Holly would pay the price. God, poor Holly. What must she be going through? That bastard Anders had better be treating her well.

"Relax. I know what I'm doing."

"I hope so." I hated having to trust a shaper to save my arse, which was basically what I was doing. Anders would never have accepted my dictating the meeting place—he'd just assume I was setting a trap for him. So I'd had to leave the choice of location to him. Most likely he'd only give me a few minutes' notice of where the handover would take place.

Which would give him plenty of time to set his own trap, the backstabbing bastard, and not much time for Steele to put his plans into motion. There wasn't much I could do on my own, unless Anders happened to choose the city zoo as his location. I should be so lucky. So I was relying on Steele to pull a rabbit out of a hat, and somehow swing it so that Holly and I both lived through the experience. Just thinking about it made me sweat even more.

Like I said, I hated relying on other people. It had rarely worked out for me in the past.

The car turned into a laneway that ran behind a high stone wall. We stopped at a large wrought-iron gate long enough for Steele to press a remote control and the gates to swing open soundlessly. I barely even noticed them closing behind us. I'd already seen it earlier, but the house that stood at the end of the long sweeping drive was no less imposing the second time around.

"I can't believe this place." It was two storeys, with the curved roof that the shapers all seemed to favour, and lit up like a Christmas tree. Glad I wasn't the one paying the power bill. "How many people live here?"

It was bigger than Alberto's pub, and looked as though it could easily house just as many people.

"Just me, and the couple who look after the place when I'm not here. Mandy cooks and cleans and David looks after the gardens."

David certainly had a full-time job on his hands. Tiny waterways snaked across the property, forming pools here and there. Bridges of stone and of wood arched prettily over the streams at intervals, and paths wound off under the trees invitingly. To my mind's eye, little sparks of life glittered here and there: birds sleeping in the trees, mostly, and a possum roaming the treetops. Some fish dreaming in the dark ponds.

The moon, almost full, sailed out from behind the clouds as Steele held the front door open for us. Worry for Holly distracted me as I walked in. She wouldn't shift until she'd given birth, but the moon being almost full would be like an itch she couldn't scratch. Last full moon, she'd been so fretful that Joe had forgone his own change to stay home with her. Anders couldn't have picked a worse time. As if she needed any other problems right now.

The foyer was large and glowed with the warmth of natural timber and woven rugs in deep shades of red and burgundy. This afternoon we'd pored over floorplans in Steele's office at the back of the house, but now he led me through to a lounge room, Syl padding silently at my side, and gestured at a couch covered in a rich brocade. Also red. After my visit to the Ruby Palace I was beginning to suspect it was every fireshaper's favourite colour.

"Take a seat," Steele said. "Are you hungry?"

It was nearly three o'clock in the morning, and I was sick with worry for Holly. The very thought of food made my stomach churn in protest.

"No, thanks." I sank gratefully into the cushioned depths of the couch and Syl leapt up and settled herself in my lap.

"Wait here. I'll get some gold."

"What for?"

"I'll need some metal if I'm going to make a copy of the ring."

I frowned. "But you don't need a spark to make fire. It just bursts right out of you." How come he couldn't just magic metal out of the air too?

"That's right." He gave me an odd look, as if he couldn't believe I didn't know this. "That's one of several reasons that fire and not metal is my primary."

He held out his hand, and it took me a moment to realise he wanted the ring. Reluctantly I placed it in his open palm. He examined it minutely, almost reverently, turning it this way and that so that it flashed in the harsh overhead lights. There was a look on his face that I'd never seen there before, almost childlike in its wonder. When he realised I was watching him, the look disappeared, replaced by his usual world-weary expression.

I let my head fall back against the couch, though I was too keyed up to sleep, and stared unseeing at the ceiling, idling stroking Syl's silky head as Steele left the room. He was back a moment later, carrying a gold bar that looked big enough to make fifty rings. Too bad you couldn't just slice a piece off.

Unless you were a metalshaper, apparently. Steele pinched one corner of the bar, and a piece peeled off in his hand as if it were soft clay. He rolled the gold between his palms until it formed a small ball.

"Catch." He threw the ball to me, then took the rest of the bar back to wherever it had come from. I was left staring at the golden marble in my hand.

It was a perfect sphere, completely cold and hard as rock. I squeezed it as hard as I could, but couldn't mar or dent it in any way. I was still marvelling at it when Steele returned and took it from me.

He sat on the opposite couch and held his hand out between us. Flames flickered in his palm around the golden ball. It melted like ice cream on a hot day and he tilted his hand, letting the gold coat his skin.

Nice party trick, said Syl.

I folded my arms. "Now you're just showing off."

He grinned, the dancing flames reflected in his eyes. "Just trying to impress the pretty lady."

He said it as if he were joking, but it occurred to me that he could have broken the chunk of gold off the bar in the other room and saved himself a trip. He probably _was_ trying to impress me with his shaping prowess by letting me see him snap it the way a normal person would break a square off a block of chocolate. A part of me preened at the idea that this undeniably gorgeous man was trying to impress me—a small part. The other part, the part that wasn't hotwired to my hormones, reeled in horror. I was not going to start _flirting_ with a shaper.

He's talking about me, right? said Syl.

I'd almost forgotten she was there. Now she abandoned me and leapt up onto the opposite couch next to Steele. Curiosity and cats: it wasn't just a saying.

How would he talking about you, furball? You've been a cat so long even I've _forgotten what you look like._

Not getting any response from me, Steele focused on his hands, turning all professional again. I ignored the unreasonable surge of disappointment, and watched as the flames and the metal began a kind of dance above his outstretched hands. How was he doing that?

I never thought that fire could be so … pretty, said Syl.

The original ring lay on the couch, not far from Syl's furry haunches, but Steele rarely glanced at it. His hands moved slowly, gracefully, through the air, as if in some slow motion martial art. The golden ball rotated slowly above them, wreathed in fire. Sweat broke out on Steele's brow as the ball spun, flattened, became first a disk, then a ring of molten metal. The flames distorted my vision of it, but I thought I saw spikes forming through the shimmering heat. How could he hold fire like that in his bare hands? The burn on my wrist throbbed in sympathy, despite the healing cream Steele had applied earlier.

I would never tell him so, but I *was* impressed, just a little. I'd seen fireshapers hurl great bolts and sheets of flame before, and been unmoved by the spectacle, but this delicate control spoke more to me of power than that kind of display, though it seemed to require just as much effort, judging by the sweat glistening on his forehead. As the flames died away, the ring, still glowing with heat, dropped to his naked palm. He never flinched, though he was breathing hard.

When he offered it to me it was cool and golden again.

"There. Gets harder all the time, but a perfect copy." He gazed on his work with a troubled look.

"Really? It gets harder? I would have thought practice made perfect."

"When the god of metalshaping dies, trust me, metalshaping gets harder and harder."

I stared back at him, hardly knowing what to say. It was no surprise that he believed in the gods—he was a shaper, after all. But to hear him speak of them as if they were real and present, not just some amorphous idea of a benevolent force watching over us, still seemed strange, despite my conversation with Alberto.

"Who is the god of metalshaping? How do you know he's dead?"

"Hephaistos." The blacksmith of the gods—the one who'd sneaked fire to Prometheus, so that mankind wouldn't die. "And I know he's dead because I saw the shadow shapers kill him."

I stared at him, my whole worldview challenged by the pain in his eyes. He believed every word he was telling me, and if this was the truth … I recalled the terrible scars on his back. I'd wondered who could possibly damage a fireshaper that way.

Perhaps a god could—or the people who had stolen a god's power.

He laughed—a short, humourless bark. "Maybe one day metalshaping will no longer be possible. But for now, I've still got it." He held the ring out to me. "No one will be able to tell the difference."

Really? I glanced between the ring in his palm and the one on the brocade couch. The one he had made was every bit as beautiful as the original, and faithfully reproduced every detail of the golden sunburst. But *I* could tell. To my mind's sight, the real ring glowed with an inner fire that tugged at wisps of memory.

My brother's face, laughing. Sunrise on a beach, the wind tossing my hair around my head in blinding strands, low clouds scudding across the sky, blanketing the rosy glow to the east. Deep in the woods, the curve of my bow a familiar weight in my hand, watching the leaves shake as my quarry moved behind the bushes.

The fake was just a ring. A beautiful ring, but no more than that. Could he really see no difference?

"As long as Anders can't tell, that's all that matters," I said.

15

There were always pigeons in the Plaza of the Sun, and the whirring of their wings formed a constant background like the shushing of the waves on a beach. This early in the morning there wasn't much traffic to drown out that sound, though there were enough people around to satisfy my requirement for a public place. I'd agreed to meet Anders here at seven.

It was ten minutes to seven, and I stood behind one of the mighty pillars of the grand post office building, watching people hurrying across the plaza on their way to work. Some tourists had arrived earlier, too—the maps they carried a dead giveaway—to see the sunrise spark on the upraised spear of Apollo.

His golden chariot was the centrepiece of the plaza, and the reason for its name. In another city, the statue would have been a grand fountain, but here in the city of the fireshapers, their homage to their god spouted flame from its wheels, and from the tip of that spear. The flames roared forth the minute the rising sun kissed the point of the god's spear, and didn't fade away again until nightfall. There was always a gaggle of tourists waiting for the sunrise with their cameras ready to catch the spectacle.

Predictably, the pigeons had lurched skyward as the flames burst forth. You'd think they'd have grown used to it after so many years, but pigeons weren't exactly mental Einsteins. They made handy little spies, however, and I'd been using them since the daylight began to grow in the plaza.

I was fully expecting Anders to have some kind of double-cross planned, so I sent the birds down every street surrounding the plaza, searching for signs: gatherings of hard-faced men, or cars that lurked suspiciously, their occupants never moving.

**Anything?* Syl asked again.

Nope.

Her tail twitched fretfully. **I don't like this.**

That made two of us. I'd have been much more comfortable if I could see where the blow was coming from. The plan was for Syl to leave as soon as I'd identified the threat, and take the news to Steele, who was waiting several blocks away with his men. Our great counterstrike wasn't going to be very effective if he had to come in blind at the last minute.

Wait. Is that them? I straightened, peering out from behind the pillar as a car pulled up outside the City Library opposite. A man and a woman got out. The woman's head was down, her long hair loose across her face, and she leaned against the man as if she were very tired, or perhaps drunk. *_That's Holly._*

And that's that lion loser with her. What's wrong with her?

Another man got out of the car and followed the other two across the plaza to the edge of the chariot. Anders. God, I'd like to punch that smug face. Syl hissed, the hairs on her back standing up like spines. She had even more reason to hate him.

It was only five to seven, but I knew Anders had seen me, though it was still dark in the shadows of the post office's long colonnade. I couldn't loiter here any longer.

_Go,_ I urged Syl. *_Are you sure you can handle it?_*

She'd promised to turn human so she could communicate with Steele.

I won't let you down. But what will I tell him?

I did a last scan of the surrounding streets, swooping dizzily from one pigeon mind to another. Still nothing. Now I wished Steele was waiting much closer, but we'd been so sure Anders would have men in the streets, and we didn't want to tip our hand too early.

I don't know. Just tell him they're here, and he'd better get his arse over here. I'll stall as long as I can.

I started the slow march down the post office steps and across the plaza as Syl slipped away. My shoes made no noise on the rough cobblestones. Half my attention was still with the birds, trying to see in every direction at once. The other half was on the face of my enemy.

Last time I'd seen Anders had been the interview where he'd made me the classic offer-you-can't-refuse. No one said no to a shaper, especially not when that shaper was on the ruling council, however junior a councillor he might be. He'd worn his robes of office then, trying to intimidate me into agreeing. And of course I had.

Foolishly, I hadn't realised he'd have me followed. The instant he knew I was running, all hell had broken loose. We'd only just managed to make it out the window of our apartment before the flames he'd sent after us destroyed the whole building. I still heard the frightened screams of our neighbours in my dreams sometimes, a shrill counterpoint to the crackle of flame. We'd been in hiding ever since, drawing the small town of Berkley's Bay around us like a cloak.

And now here we were. It hadn't taken him that long to ferret us out after all. He watched me cross the plaza toward him with his hands in the trouser pockets of his expensive suit. No council robes today. He looked like any of half a dozen businessmen who'd already passed us, briefcases in hand. I'd wondered if he would even come, or whether he'd leave it all to Mason. Apparently the lure of the ring was too strong—or maybe he just didn't trust Mason enough.

Holly suddenly lurched to one side, almost doubled over, and Mason pushed her roughly down onto the low stone wall that kept the tourists from getting too close to Apollo and his flaming chariot.

"What have you done to her?" I snapped.

Anders spread his hands, a look of mock innocence on his face. "I? I've done nothing. This was done some months ago—about nine, most likely."

I glanced sharply at Holly, who met my gaze through the sweaty strands of her hair. She clutched her enormous belly, a strained look on her face.

"You're in labour?"

She nodded, and bit her lip.

"When did it start?"

When she didn't answer, Anders shrugged. "Some time in the night. For your sake, I hope it wasn't too long ago. I certainly wouldn't want to be midwife at a werewolf birth. You're liable to get your head bitten off. Literally."

So he was still pretending I was going to walk out of here alive. Could he possibly be sincere? A little bubble of hope rose inside me. I hadn't seen any sign of the anticipated double-cross.

But this was the man who'd set fire to a whole apartment building, knowing full well that there were innocent people inside, knowing and not caring in the slightest whether they made it out alive. The bubble burst as swiftly as it had formed. I was no child, to believe in happy endings. I knew better than to trust the word of shapers.

"I heard all the commotion last night at the palace," he continued conversationally, as if we were two old mates who'd just happened to run into each other beside the chariot. "I'd heard you were good, of course, but I must admit I'm impressed you managed to pull it off."

"All part of the service." I had to force myself to speak politely. I'd rather have spit on him than spend another minute in his company, but the pigeons showed me a convoy of provost cars on their way here, and I was supposed to be stalling him.

"Let's see it, then."

His eyes, reflecting Apollo's flames, were alight with hunger. I reached into my back pocket and pulled out the ring, holding it up to catch the light. Flames seemed to dance across the golden surface. He held out his hand, imperious.

"Nuh-uh." I shook my head, backing away. "Not so fast. Holly, can you walk?"

For answer, she shook off Mason's restraining hand and lurched to her feet. She was panting, and her eyes had a faraway look, as if all her energy was focused inward. Her hands rested lightly on her belly, and I saw it ripple with the power of her contraction. Exactly how far away was that baby?

"Go join that group of tourists." A dozen or so people still lingered on the other side of the chariot, taking group shots with the flaming Apollo in the background. Holly circled obediently around the low stone wall.

Anders clicked his fingers at me. "My patience is wearing thin."

"Then it's all yours." I tossed the ring into the flames and ran to join Holly. He cursed and hurdled the wall to save it. A fireshaper like him wouldn't be hurt by the flames, though the ring might. Hopefully he'd be distracted long enough for us to get away.

"Hurry," said Holly. "I'm between contractions."

She headed for the closest side street, setting an impressive pace for a woman in labour, and I ran after her. We earned some curious glances from the tourists.

I looked back. Mason was watching us, but hadn't moved. Strange. I'd expected him to give chase, even if Anders was busy. We were almost to the edge of the plaza when three provosts in riot gear burst out of the side street. More came from every street that opened onto the plaza, until a force of about twenty loosely circled the chariot. The tourists stirred in alarm, as flighty as the pigeons. Anders and Mason stood rooted to the spot.

"You can stop now," I said, putting a hand out to halt Holly's headlong charge. "These guys are with us."

Steele strode out into the plaza, hot as ever in tight black

T-shirt and jeans. No riot gear for him. It was probably the first time in my life I'd ever been happy to see a shaper.

"Is that Jake Steele?" Holly asked. "What's *he* doing here?"

"Believe it or not, he's helping us."

Steele motioned for the provosts to let the tourists leave. A gap opened up in the circle and they were bustled away. They didn't go far, though, only joining the crowd that was starting to form around the perimeter of the plaza. The Plaza of the Sun wasn't usually this exciting. No one wanted to miss the action.

A familiar black cat sauntered up to us and rubbed her head against Holly's leg.

You didn't stay human for long.

I don't think I'll feel secure as a human until that douchebag is in jail.

Well, shouldn't be long now. Screw not gloating over your enemy's downfall. I'd hardly dared to dream that such a moment would ever come, and I planned to enjoy every minute of it. If that made me a bad person, so be it.

A hush fell over the plaza as Steele stopped in front of Anders.

"Councillor Anders, you're in possession of stolen property." His voice wasn't loud, but I heard him. All my senses were focused on this moment.

"You mean this little trinket?" Anders wore the ring

now, and he held up his hand to display it. "I'm afraid you've got me. Caught red-handed."

Steele paused. He probably hadn't expected an insta-confession. Anders' mocking tone bothered me too. Did he think he'd get out of this just because he had friends in high places? The Ruby Adept was his chief supporter on the council, and he was hardly likely to be impressed that his protégé had arranged to steal a ring of power from him.

Steele gestured to one of the provosts. "Captain, arrest Councillor Anders."

The wall of provosts stood unmoving, shields up, guns at the ready.

"Whoops," said Anders. "I don't think he heard you."

Uh-oh. Everything changed in a millisecond. The smirk on Anders' face, the provosts standing in rigid silence—the bottom was still falling out of my stomach as my brain caught up with the realisation that we'd been betrayed. I screamed a warning to Steele and started running, but he was too far away. I couldn't get to him in time. So I reached for a flock of the ever-present pigeons and hurled them straight at the provosts.

The captain brought his gun up, but a pigeon smacked him in the face as he fired. Steele jerked as the bullet thudded into him, then he sent a sheet of flame roaring across the plaza.

"Jake, no!" I fought my way into the storm of pigeons. "Look out for the tourists!"

The air filled with screams and singed feathers. Clouds of steam boiled skyward as Anders met Steele's fire with a wall of water. Maybe there *were* times when it was useful to be a fireshaper with a water secondary. Too late to save most of the provosts, though. Their blackened shapes on the ground reeked of burnt flesh and sour smoke. I choked, gagging on the smell. It was that night in the apartment all over again, as if I were trapped in a recurring nightmare where people burned because of me.

Jake's blue gaze met mine for an instant amongst the chaos, and then he staggered, nearly dropping to his knees. Bright blood ran down his arm as he snatched up the riot shield of a fallen provost. Shapers, for all their power, weren't immune to bullets.

Flames of his own burst from Anders' hands, and he raised them high. I renewed my aerial assault on him, doing my best to ignore the smell of roast bird and the pitiful burnt pigeons littering the ground. A handful of provosts clustered behind him, momentarily too distracted by the dive-bombing pigeons to take any further part in the battle. They were all that was left of the twenty who had marched into the plaza a moment before. I had less pity for them than for the birds.

Jake summoned fire, too, though it wasn't as impressive as his first blast, which had scorched deep black grooves into the cobblestones all the way to the edge of the plaza.

Blood dripped from his fingers, and fear clutched at my heart.

"Get Holly to safety," he yelled at me. I ignored him, of course. There was no way I could leave him there, even if he was a shaper—though I was fast running out of pigeons. That bastard Anders was searing them from the sky. "Go!"

"You're hurt." I had to shout to be heard above the roaring of flame and the screams of the onlookers. Somewhere in the distance, I thought I heard a siren's wail. "Come with me! I'll hold him off." *While there are still birds left. Come on, Jake, please.*

For answer, he turned his flames on the great statue of Apollo.

"What are you doing? Let's go!" My throat hurt from screaming in the smoke-filled air.

Jake's flames danced over the statue's surface, his arms held out to it almost in entreaty. They shook with effort.

A great metallic grinding shrieked through the smoke, and the ground beneath my feet shuddered. I blinked my watering eyes, sure I was seeing things.

Apollo turned his huge bronze head. His horses tossed their heads and stomped their massive hooves with the sound of a hammer striking an anvil. The chariot rumbled into life, ploughing straight through the low wall surrounding it. Stone blocks the size of my head tumbled aside like pebbles.

Anders' flames winked out in a heartbeat. His mouth fell open as the god drew back his mighty arm, his spear tip pointed unwaveringly at the traitorous shaper. Anders backed away, slowly at first, then faster as the chariot began to pick up speed.

Jake collapsed to the buckled ground just as Anders turned and sprinted for the edge of the plaza, the surviving provosts hurtling after him, the bronze god in lumbering pursuit.

"Can't … keep it up … much longer," Jake ground out through gritted teeth.

I hauled him to his feet, tucking myself under his good arm. "Then let's get out of here while Apollo's still got our backs."

My car was only a few blocks away, but I doubted he could make it that far. Holly met me as we staggered into the nearest side street, and an almighty clang made me look back over my shoulder. Apollo's massive bronze spear was embedded into a building on the far side of the plaza. I hoped Jake was as rich as I thought. There was going to be one hell of a clean-up bill from this little fiasco.

Apollo was still moving, but only at a walking pace. I couldn't see Anders and his men through the clearing smoke, but it was obvious that Jake's metalshaping was nearly at an end. It looked as though Apollo would roll to a halt right in the mouth of one of the streets that fed onto the plaza. Peak hour traffic might be a little more challenging than usual this morning.

Time for us to be somewhere else. Jake swayed on his feet, and Holly didn't look much better.

"Wait here." I ran back into the plaza and grabbed a chunk of stone.

What are you— Syl stopped as I smashed the window of the nearest car. **Oh, damn, I thought so.**

You got any better ideas? I threw Syl a dirty look as I helped Jake into the passenger seat. **You going to turn human and help me carry these two three blocks through the city with Anders on our tails?**

How are you going to start it, genius? You think people leave their keys handily placed for thieves?

I brushed broken glass from the driver's seat. **Get in the back with Holly and make yourself useful.**

"Jake!" I patted his cheek, none too gently. "You still with us?"

His head lolled back against the seat, but he opened his eyes at the sound of my voice.

"I need one more magic trick from you, all right?" His face was so pale it scared me, but I kept my voice cheerful.

"I'm not your performing monkey, woman." Well, he wasn't dead yet. He still had his shaper ego intact.

I pulled my own keyring from my pocket and ripped a key off it. "Shape this so it starts this car."

His fingers trembled as they closed around the key. After a moment he shoved the key at me and closed his eyes again.

Turned out my hand was shaking, too. It took me three tries to get the damned key into the ignition, watching the plaza in the rear vision mirror the whole time in case Anders and his goons reappeared. Sirens wailed louder now. The noise seemed to be coming from all sides. In the back seat Holly moaned softly.

As I pulled out, I heard a scream of rage behind us. I looked out my smashed window and saw a figure emerge from the smoke, running hard in our direction. Anders.

I gunned the motor and took off with a squeal of tyres.

What's his problem? Syl asked. **He got what he wanted.**

I guess he figured out it wasn't the real thing.

16

What had Jake said about the gods laughing at the plans of mortals? I was no longer so sure the gods weren't real, but if I were a true believer, I'd be royally pissed with them about now.

I'd only driven five minutes before stopping at a supermarket to buy basic first-aid supplies. Jake was bleeding like a stuck pig in the front seat, and Holly could well be bleeding in the back seat before long. I picked up an armful of towels, too, just in case.

Can't we just drop these two at the nearest hospital? Syl asked as I threw the supplies in the back with her.

I'd love to. I really would have. I knew nothing about labour or babies, and Anders' comments about the danger of being around a labouring werewolf had struck a chord. Usually shifters gave birth surrounded by their own kind, who could help them stay in control—or deal with the consequences if they couldn't. But how could I dump Holly among strangers and skip town? What was I going to do then? Ring Joe and say, *Hi, I just left your missing wife at a random hospital, and she may or may not have given birth to your baby by the time you get there?* I wouldn't be able to look at myself in the mirror any more.

As for Jake, that got even more complicated. Anders was still on the loose, and clearly he had more allies than Jake knew about. Even leaving him at his own house could be signing his death warrant. He seemed oddly weak, even considering the shoulder wound. Had the effort of animating the giant statue weakened him beyond recovery? If metalshaping was so hard that even creating the fake ring had been an effort, how much more must animating that much metal have taken out of him?

His head lolled against the seat, his face grey with exhaustion. I longed to help him, but I knew so little about shapers—I had no idea what to do. One thing was for sure: he was in no condition to defend himself. I couldn't risk leaving him.

But it's not safe, I told her. **And we need to get Holly back to Berkley's Bay. Back to Joe.**

What about Hot Stuff?

He'll have to come along for the ride.

There was a good hospital in Berkley's Bay. Alberto was there, too. He'd know what to do. Ever since I'd met him,

I'd had a good feeling about Alberto. I was sure he'd be able to help us. He could hide Jake, if it came to that. And I knew I could count on him if Anders came calling.

Not that I expected Anders to show up. Berkley's Bay was the last place I should be going. Given our mutual history, he was more likely to assume I'd pull another disappearing act.

I started the car, and Syl grudgingly took human form after I pointed out that I couldn't drive the car, bandage Jake, *and* help a woman in labour all at the same time. I was good, but not that good. Syl leaned awkwardly through the front seats and rigged a temporary bandage for Jake's shoulder while I drove.

"I don't think it's as bad as it looks," she said. "There's a lot of blood, but the bullet's gone straight through. Once we can get him cleaned up, he won't look so much like the walking dead."

"I think it's more than that." I risked a quick glance at him. If anything, he looked worse, but I didn't tell her about the metalshaping problem. I had a feeling that information wasn't meant for sharing. "I think he's got some kind of shaper sickness."

"Damn." She brushed his sweaty hair off his face. "Just when I was starting to like him."

"Let's not write him off just yet. Alberto might be able to help."

Perhaps my faith in Alberto was just wishful thinking,

but with the situation rapidly going from bad to worse, I needed something positive to hold onto. I kept an eye on Holly in the rear vision mirror. She was flushed, her hair limp and stuck to her face with sweat, and I could tell she was gritting her teeth against the pain.

"How far apart are those contractions, Holly?"

"Don't. Know. Closer … than before."

Just what I needed to hear.

"I'll time it," Syl said. "Tell me when the next one starts, all right?"

I finally made it to the highway. It was peak hour, but all the traffic was on the other side of the road, heading into the city. Some of the kinks in my neck unwound as I hit the open road. I could finally put some distance between me and Anders—although telling myself he was unlikely to be following didn't stop me from compulsively checking the road behind me. Still clear.

Syl and Holly were occupied in the back seat. I glanced across at Jake, who still had his eyes shut. Asleep or unconscious? At least he was a better colour now. I reached across and tapped his bare arm. No response.

Good. I slid my hand into the front pocket of his jeans. It was kind of awkward with him slumped over the way he was, and me with one hand on the wheel and half an eye on the road. But I knew he'd have it with him. He wouldn't have risked leaving it somewhere.

And I was right. My fingers touched something cool and metallic. Gradually, I wormed it out of those tight-fitting jeans and closed my fist around it.

"What are you doing?" Syl asked as I drew my hand back. She had to raise her voice to be heard above the wind buffeting through my smashed window now we'd picked up some speed.

"Just checking the bandages. He's fine."

If she'd noticed that my hand hadn't been anywhere near the bandages, she said nothing, distracted by a groan from Holly.

"I can't believe it *hurts* this much," Holly panted. "Why does it have to hurt? It's supposed to be a natural process."

"More proof that God is not a woman," Syl said, using one of the towels to wipe Holly's dripping face. Holly growled and shoved her hand away. I had no idea what kind of gods, if any, werewolves worshipped. In any case, Holly wasn't in the mood for religious debates.

I shoved the ring deep into my own pocket and checked the rear vision mirror again. No sign of pursuit. In the back seat, Syl had left a bigger gap between herself and the labouring werewolf.

"Sorry. It'll feel like … bad period pain, they said." Holly bit her words off as the next contraction hit. "Period pain … my arse."

Then the words disappeared altogether, replaced by a whimper of agony.

Syl leaned forward, speaking right into my ear. "They're only a minute apart now. Do you think the baby's coming?"

I met her eyes in the mirror. Neither of us knew the first thing about this. We were way out of our depth.

"We should ring Joe," Syl said. Holly didn't give any sign of recognition at the mention of her husband's name, if she even heard it over the rush of wind. Her eyes were closed, her face tight with pain as she panted.

"Joe? What use is he going to be?" Maybe if he were here, but over the phone?

"He went to those shifter antenatal classes with her, didn't he? He must know more than we do."

Just about everyone would know more about it than we did, but I was getting the uneasy feeling that lack of knowledge wasn't going to be our main problem. Holly's eyes had a wild look to them that didn't bode well.

"Lie down," Syl urged, her face pale. "Try to rest in between contractions."

Holly snarled. "You try resting with someone sticking knives into your gut."

She tore impatiently at the button on her maternity jeans, as if she couldn't bear the touch of the fabric any more. The look on her face alarmed me.

"Holly, stay human," I said sharply.

She struggled out of her jeans as fluid gushed all over the seat.

"Oh, hell, her water's broken," Syl said.

"Stay calm. That doesn't mean anything. It could still be hours." So I'd heard, anyway. I checked the clock on the dash. Maybe another two hours until we reached Berkley's Bay. Less if I put my foot down.

"Hours? I can't do this for *hours*. Oh, God." Holly knelt up on the wet seat, clutching the back of it. Her head banged against the rear window of the car but she didn't seem to notice.

"That's good," said Syl. "Lean your body against the back of the seat like that. It's supposed to be better to stay upright, isn't it? So gravity can help?"

I didn't know who she was asking, because I had no idea and Holly wasn't listening. She screamed and grunted, such animal sounds that I had to keep checking she was still human. Jake stirred, roused at last by all the noise.

He glanced into the back seat, then turned his gaze resolutely forward. "Where are we going?"

"Berkley's Bay."

"How much longer?"

"Couple of hours, tops."

"We need help."

"Indeed. If you have any hidden baby-delivering skills, now would be the time to reveal them."

But my sarcasm was wasted. His eyes had slid closed again. Damn. Worry for him leapfrogged to the top of my list of problems again. How much blood had he lost, exactly? Or was it just the effort of animating that enormous statue that had worn him out?

The needle on the speedo crept higher. I couldn't get to Berkley's Bay soon enough.

The next hour was a nightmare. I tried to focus on the road but the agonised sounds coming from the back seat were horribly distracting. Syl kept up a steady stream of encouragement, but Holly seemed beyond hearing her. Maybe it just made Syl feel like she was being of some use.

But really there was nothing any of us could do. Holly's body had to do the work on its own. We were maybe fifteen minutes out of Berkley's Bay when it became obvious that it couldn't. Holly was scrunched up against the car door, knees up, legs spread wide. The contractions were coming so fast there was hardly any break between them, and she was grunting like an animal in pain.

"There's blood on the seat," Syl shouted, panic in her voice.

"There's always blood," I said, as if I knew what I was talking about, but I turned around for a quick look anyway. The back seat looked like the scene of a massacre. "Just hang on. We're nearly there."

But not nearly enough.

"I keep *pushing*," Holly panted, "but nothing's *happening*." She finished on a wail that turned into a howl.

"Oh, no you don't!" I pulled off the highway with a screech of brakes that sent the gravel of the shoulder spraying from under my tyres. "Holly, you have to stay human!"

I flung open the car door and was hit by the smell of petrol and burnt rubber. I yanked Syl's door open.

"You drive."

Syl scrambled out, only too happy to leave Holly to me. I climbed in to find thick dark hairs sprouting on Holly's arms and bare legs.

"Holly! Stay with me!"

But she couldn't hear me, lost in pain. Her wolf was frightened and it wanted out. Faster than you could say *My, what big teeth you have*, I was sharing the back seat with a terrified wolf that would be only too happy to spread that pain around.

Syl took off with a squeal of tyres, and I lurched toward the wolf. It snarled at me, all its hackles standing up.

Holly! I slammed into her mind. Rude of me, I know, but the situation was about to turn ugly. **Holly, get a grip! I know it hurts, but you need to let me help you.**

"Umm, Lexi?" Syl said. "I think we're being followed."

17

I risked a quick peek out the back window. There was a car back there, not close enough to identify the people in it, but moving a lot faster than the speed limit.

Damn it. We were so close to safety. But I couldn't think about it with a werewolf writhing and howling on the seat next to me. Her claws were ripping into my legs even through my jeans. I certainly wouldn't be able to help her while she was in this state.

Holly, come on. There's no way you can push a human baby out of a wolf's body. Just thinking about the logistics of that made me wince. This child wouldn't be able to shapeshift until it was a couple of years old at least. I just hoped its mother changing forms hadn't harmed it. **You've got to change back.**

The wolf shook her head, as if she could dislodge me from her mind that way. She squinted her yellow eyes against the rush of wind from the broken driver's window and growled at me. I persisted, talking to her through the link until the crazy faded from her eyes and she finally answered.

Is that you, Lexi? How are you doing that?

Never mind now. Long story. Right now I need you to take human form again so I can help you have this baby. I don't want to lose a hand here.

The wolf's body shivered back into human shape. Holly half-lay across the seat, panting.

"Let me have a look." That was what they did in the movies, right? And then they popped up and said in a cheery voice, *I can see the head! Not much longer now.*

And I *could* see a head, just the very top of it, smeared with blood and gunk. Another contraction seized Holly. Her face went bright red as she pushed, but that little head didn't budge.

Holly collapsed against the seat, panting, when the contraction was over. "It's stuck, isn't it?"

"I've heard that first babies can take a long time." Maybe this was all perfectly normal. How the hell would I know?

I checked out the back window again. The car, a dark four-wheel drive, was a lot closer now. I recognised the farmland on either side of the road. The turn-off to Berkley's Bay wasn't far now.

"Go faster, Syl."

"What?" The wind buffeting through her broken window made it hard for her to hear.

"Faster!"

"I don't think I can." She clutched the wheel so tightly her knuckles were white.

The back window shattered and the car swerved wildly as Syl jerked the wheel in surprise.

"Are they shooting at us?" she screamed, her voice coloured with equal parts disbelief and outrage. The car leapt forward as she discovered that, actually, she *could* go faster. Holly and I were littered with fragments of safety glass; I brushed them off as best I could.

Poor Holly was oblivious, lost in her own world of pain.

"You've got to get it out, Lexi. I can't stand it!"

Holy hell. This was a nightmare. I leaned through the seats and shook Jake roughly. He'd stirred when Syl had thrown him against the door with her wild manoeuvres, but he was still groggy.

"Jake! Wake up! We need you."

I nearly fell off the seat as Syl swerved again, though no one was firing at us anymore.

"Ice!" she screamed. "There's ice on the road. Hold on!"

The car fishtailed wildly. Holly and I were thrown around the back seat like balls in a pinball machine. Ice? Warm spring sunshine was beating down outside. Where the hell had ice come from?

Jake roused, and flame leapt from his fingertips through the open window. Syl jerked her head back in surprise as fire licked past her nose. Clouds of steam boiled up from the road surface as Jake's flames dissolved the ice.

He swivelled around in his seat, then threw a fireball out the gaping hole where the back window had been. It made a very satisfying *whump!* as it exploded on the car behind us. I stuck my head up long enough to see Anders hanging out the passenger side window, putting out flames with a stream of water from the irrigation ditches in the fields that were flashing past.

Holly wailed like a soul in torment, flinging her head from side to side. "Get it *out*. Get it *out*."

If Jake's gods were watching, I hoped they helped me now. I huddled between her knees, trying to get my fingers around the slippery little head. There was a lot of blood. I didn't want to add to Holly's pain, but there's just no delicate way of getting your hand inside someone else's body.

"Throw some more fireballs," I urged Jake, my fingers already cramping at the odd position. The baby's head was so tiny, and I was terrified of hurting it. "Keep them occupied. We're nearly there."

Even as I spoke, Syl took the turn-off to town, tyres squealing. Jake threw another fireball, but it was smaller than the last, and he was sweating with effort, his face so pale he looked like he was about to pass out. But I couldn't worry about him now. I was sweating too, with the responsibility of delivering this baby safely. I pulled gently, trying to guide the baby's head.

Another contraction rocked Holly, rippling across her distended belly.

"Push now," I said. "As hard as you can. I'll pull."

Holly grunted with effort, a sound that bordered on a growl. Hair sprouted on her legs. I slapped her face hard, leaving a bloody handprint on her cheek.

"Stay human," I snapped. "You can *do* this, Holly."

We needed some werewolves here, to help her control herself. We needed Joe. If only I had another pair of hands I could ring him. But I was fully occupied with Holly, Jake was focused on fighting off Anders' attacks, and Syl had her hands full keeping the car on the road. Anders kept trying with the ice, though so far Jake had managed to melt everything he threw at us. There was no point in him pitting his own flames against Jake's, since he was a weaker fireshaper—although if Jake's strength kept fading he might stand a chance.

He seemed to come to the same conclusion. A fireball came so close before Jake batted it away that I felt scorching heat all down my arm and the side of my face through the gaping hole of the back window. The smell of burnt hair hung in the air. My skin prickled with heat, as if I'd spent all day laying in the sun.

I glanced at Jake with real alarm. Sweat streamed down his ashen face.

"Too close, Jake! Melt their car or something."

He gritted his teeth and diverted another fireball. "Not enough. Power. Left."

As we rocketed down the main street of town I felt a rush of warmth over my hands. Holly was pushing again, the veins in her forehead standing out with the effort. The warmth on my hands was her blood.

She'd torn, but the head was out.

"Almost there, Holly. You're doing great."

She nodded, too exhausted to speak.

We roared past the supermarket, the four-wheel drive right on our tail.

"Where to?" Syl asked. "I can't shake them."

If only it wasn't daytime, I'd run to Alberto. There weren't many shifters that could take on a shaper, but I reckoned Alberto had a fighting chance against Anders. But it was ten o'clock in the morning. Bright daylight, so Alberto wasn't an option. We'd have to rely on our own resources.

"Home," I said. "Let's get Holly and her baby to Joe."

The speeding cars were turning heads all down the street. People came out of shops to look as we passed. But it wasn't the people I was interested in. I began to reach out, gathering those "resources" with my mind even as I nodded encouragement at Holly.

"One more big push. Time to meet your baby."

She reached down, felt the damp head. It seemed to give her renewed determination. When the contraction seized her she bore down with all her remaining strength. After all those hours of effort, the last bit seemed almost easy. The baby slithered out onto the back seat in a rush of blood and other fluid.

Oh, my God. It was so tiny, so red and wrinkled and perfect.

"It's a girl." My eyes met Holly's in a shared moment of joy and wonder that ended abruptly as the car behind rammed us.

I grabbed for the baby as we were all jolted forward. Syl screamed and stomped on the brake. Not one of her better ideas. The car hit us again and we were shunted sideways. I clutched the tiny body against my chest, bracing myself against the back of the seat in front. We spun through three hundred and sixty degrees and slammed sideways into a wall with a noise like the end of the world.

Okay, so maybe it was a good thing after all that Syl had braked.

It took me a long moment to realise we'd stopped. My ears were ringing. I looked down at the baby in my arms, still attached by the cord to its mother. It opened dark, slitted eyes and gazed up at me in indignation. Then it opened its mouth and wailed, a high-pitched cry that sounded more like something that should have come out of a kitten's mouth than a human's.

"You okay?" I asked Holly, and she nodded, reaching for the baby. "Syl? Jake?"

Syl groaned, but Jake lay still. I shook him, heart in my mouth. He didn't *look* hurt, but there'd been something wrong ever since the fight in the plaza. Lucky he was a shaper, and I didn't care whether he lived or died.

I shook the bastard harder. I was a terrible liar. Even *I* thought so. Somehow in the last twenty-four hours of fighting with him and fighting alongside him (and maybe even during the kissing bit, if I was really honest with myself) I'd come to care what happened to one shaper, at least.

Someone wrenched open the door next to me with a shriek of metal. A gun appeared in the opening.

"Out," said a voice.

I obeyed, staggering a little as I found my feet. The hand holding the gun belonged to Mason, the lion shifter. Behind me, Holly groaned. There was still the placenta to deliver. I risked a look back and saw a black cat dart away from the wreck. The car sat half on the footpath and half on the street, rammed up against the pub. Alberto was not going to be pleased at those cracks in his façade when he woke tonight.

"Move." Mason prodded me away from the car. I put

my hands up and moved. Anders stood in the middle of the road, wreathed in fire, a smug expression on his face.

The street, which had been full of people, rapidly emptied at sight of the fireshaper. No one interfered with shaper justice in a shaper town. Syl would find Joe, and the wolves would come, but even they wouldn't take on a shaper in a straight fight.

Luckily I had a few tricks up my sleeve. This fight would be as dirty as they came.

18

Did I mention that Berkley's Bay was a seaside town? Seagulls were always hanging around, stealing food from the tourists, squawking and fighting over every scrap of fish from the trawlers, and generally crapping on everything like pigeons on steroids. For the last few minutes I'd been gathering a storm of seagulls—a veritable tornado of seagulls—ready to drop on Anders' unsuspecting but very deserving head.

Admittedly, the fire would be a problem for them, and I felt bad about that, but there was a time for soft and fluffy animal love, and there was a time for protecting what mattered. Holly and her baby needed me. *Jake* needed me. Some time when I had more time to think about that, I'd be all kinds of screwed up about feeling protective of a shaper. I didn't know quite what I felt for that hot flamethrower, but I'd walk over burning coals to save him from Anders.

Although, come to think of it, I'd walk over burning coals to save my worst enemy from Anders. Assuming I had an enemy worse than Anders himself, that is. And I had no time to analyse my feelings for a certain blue-eyed shaper, with Anders smirking at me like that. He was tossing something up in the air, then catching it in one flaming hand, over and over—something that glinted gold in the morning sun as it tumbled through the air. Its twin rode in my pocket even now.

"It's quite a good copy, you know," he said conversationally. The ring flashed and turned in the air. "If it hadn't started to melt in that fire you threw it into, I might have gone on believing it was the real thing for some time. I must compliment Steele before I kill him."

"What are you talking about?" Might as well keep him talking. It would give Joe more time to get here.

"This ring you gave me. It's not the original."

I shrugged. "You said get the ring from the Ruby Adept's safe. That's it. Maybe he didn't know it was a copy."

"You think the Ruby Adept wouldn't be able to tell the difference between a fake and the avatar of Apollo?"

The avatar of Apollo? Holy shit. That sounded kind of serious.

"So maybe he kept it as a decoy, and the real one's somewhere else."

A black cat poked its head around the corner of a building behind Anders.

"Bullshit. You know how many metalshapers could make a copy of that ring?"

"Probably most of them."

What's happening, Syl? Between Anders and keeping the seagulls at the ready, I didn't want to split my attention too many ways. I just needed a quick update. **Found Joe yet?**

We're in the alley next to Tegan's salon. Tegan's here too, and Norma and Ray are on their way.

Anders moved closer and I took an involuntary step back, my eyes on those flames.

"Since Hephaistos was killed? Probably only a handful of them," he said. "And do you know how many of those came to the Plaza this morning to arrest me?" He took another step closer. "Just the one."

Behind me, the baby cried again. No other sound. Now would be a really good time for Jake to wake up and light a fire under Anders, but it didn't seem like I was going to get that wish. Shifters and seagulls were better than nothing, but I'd have felt more confident about taking on Anders with a shaper on my side.

Time to stop stalling and bite the bullet, before he and his flames got any closer to the people I was trying to protect. Nobody else was going to die in a fireshaper's flames because of me.

"Okay, you got me. Jake copied the ring and palmed off the fake on you."

"And where's the real one?"

"In the Ruby Adept's safe, where it should be. You're in kind of a lot of trouble, actually. I don't think your boss is very happy with you."

It was like standing in front of a bonfire. The parts of me that faced him stung with heat, while my back was cold. My burned wrist throbbed in sympathy, reminding me just how nasty it could be to get on a fireshaper's bad side. This tête-à-tête was getting too hot to handle. I sent the call out to my gathered flock.

"I hope for your sake you're lying," he said. "If I don't get that ring right now, a lot of people are going to die, starting with your werewolf friend."

That was it. I was done taking shit from fireshapers. I dropped a frothing whirlwind of sharp beaks and frenzied wings on his head.

He threw up his arms, shooting flames into the sky, but some got through. The noise was unbelievable: the roar of flame, the thunder of wings, the raucous screeching of hundreds of seagulls. Mason started shooting, so I threw some birds at him too, and he dropped his gun to cover his face and head instead.

Joe and Tegan burst from the alley. Tegan made a beeline for the car, but Joe stopped to deliver a punch that dropped Mason like a stone.

"Get Holly out of here!" I shouted over the uproar, and he nodded, his face grim. I wondered how much Syl had told him of what his wife had been through.

I lunged for Mason's gun, but a bolt of fire melted it to slag before I could reach it. I danced back as another bolt seared the ground at my feet. A few brave birds still dive-bombed Anders, but most had either fled or lay smoking on the street.

I glanced wildly around. Joe had Holly in his arms, while Tegan carried their tiny newborn. Anders threw a wall of flame that stopped the little group in its tracks. He had white feathers in his hair, and a pissed-off expression on his blood-streaked face.

"Last chance," he said. "Give me the ring."

I cast around for allies, but animals are smart. All the locals had fled the scene of the battle. None were close enough to help me now. I had the feeling Anders wouldn't wait much longer. But what could I do? If I gave him the ring, he'd still kill everyone. There seemed no way out.

Anders' wall of flame flickered and faded out as Jake staggered from the car, pale as a reanimated corpse.

"Run," he snapped.

Joe and Tegan ran, not waiting to be told twice, but I stayed where I was.

Come* on.* Syl was nowhere in sight but her voice in my head was clear enough. **Do as the man says.

He can barely stand, I objected. **Anders will kill him.**

A little bubble of panic rose in my throat. I couldn't leave Jake to face Anders alone. Anders would never have been able to take him under normal circumstances, and I wasn't letting the backstabbing little snake beat him now, just because Jake had tried to help me. It had nothing to do with the fact that my heart beat a little faster every time I saw Jake, or that his presence seemed to light up a room. I was just protecting a friend. I would have done the same for Syl, or Joe, or Holly.

Anders hurled a fireball, which Jake somehow turned and sent hurtling back at him.

He seems to be doing all right, Syl pointed out. **Get out of there and let the shaper bastards fight it out.**

But she couldn't see the way Jake's raised arms were trembling, or how the sweat trickled down his pale face. Maybe he was a shaper bastard, or maybe there was more to him than that, but I couldn't just *leave* him.

I edged closer to Jake. "Distract him."

"Trying."

He shot a series of fiery thunderbolts at Anders that sizzled in flight. Mason was up again, crawling towards their car. He seemed no threat; I could deal with him later. I waited until Anders was busy deflecting the bolts, then whipped out my first knife and hurled it at him. Anders yelped as the blade lodged in his shoulder. Mason crawled faster. Score one for me.

Jake sagged against me as I released the second knife, sending it veering off course. It clattered against a building. And then his flames winked out as he collapsed to his knees.

"Jake!" I grabbed at him before he could topple onto his face, kneeling on the street by his side.

"Very touching," said Anders, a vicious satisfaction in his eyes as he watched me struggle to support Jake's weight. "But you should have run when he told you to. Who's going to save you now?"

He sent a pillar of fire blasting into the sky, and I hid my face in Jake's hair, waiting for the end.

And so I didn't see the doors of the pub burst off their hinges and fly across the street, although I sure heard the boom, followed by the clatter of the door frames and the odd brick hitting the ground. When I looked up, Alberto stood there, dapper as ever, not a hair out of place.

"Actually, that would be me," he said.

My mouth fell open. Brick dust and darkness boiled around him, and I glimpsed shapes in the smoke—strange, distorted figures. Eyes glinted, appearing and disappearing like visions as black tendrils writhed outward, reaching toward Anders.

I coughed, choking on dust. My eyes watered. Surely I was seeing things? Alberto was cloaked in night, black as the pits of hell—at ten o'clock on a bright sunny morning.

Gunfire shattered the air. Mason leaned on the open

door of the four-wheel drive, firing at Alberto across the top. The gun must have been in the car. Anders, shrugging off his shock at Alberto's dramatic entrance, joined in, pelting him with fireballs.

Alberto stalked toward them. Neither bullets nor fireballs had any effect on him. He simply kept walking.

Jake cocked an eyebrow at me. "I thought he was a vampire?"

His voice held a hint of accusation, as if I'd been keeping things from him. Well, I *was* keeping things from him—the ring in my pocket burned like a guilty secret—but nothing about Alberto.

"Yeah, me too." I put an arm around his broad shoulders, suddenly more hopeful of living through this experience than I'd been in quite some time.

Alberto stopped in front of Mason, who couldn't seem to stop squeezing the trigger though he'd long since run out of bullets. His face was frozen in a mask of horror as the black tendrils swirled languidly around him. Alberto raised his hand and plunged it into the lion shifter's chest. There was no sound, no blood—but when Alberto withdrew his hand, Mason collapsed at his feet, deader than dead.

I caught my breath; it seemed the whole world stopped breathing. Alberto looked at Anders. Just looked at him, nothing more, but it was enough to send Anders spinning away, running for his life.

It made no difference. Alberto flowed after him, wreathed in living darkness, and engulfed the fleeing figure. A scream choked off and I turned away, hiding my face again in Jake's neck.

He smelled of smoke and tasted like salt. His arms came around me and I felt myself truly relax for the first time since the night Syl and I had fled the city all those months ago. Anders was finally dead, and those encircling arms felt like a promise.

"Did you just *lick* me?" Jake asked, lazy amusement in his voice.

"Of course not." I pushed him away. "You must be delirious."

His blue eyes smiled down at me from a face covered in grime and sweat. "You have that effect on me."

Suddenly, I had trouble breathing. Probably all that smoke in the air. Despite the dirt, he was the best thing I'd seen all day. We'd made it. I gazed back at him, aware I was grinning like an idiot, but somehow unable to wipe the smile from my face.

Behind us someone cleared their throat. It was Alberto, minus the scary writhing blackness. The smiling Alberto I was used to, except that …

"Alberto, how are you still standing there?" I asked. "It's broad daylight. Shouldn't you have burnt to dust by now?"

He looked almost embarrassed as he helped me to my

feet. "I suppose I can't hide it anymore," he said. "I'm not actually a vampire."

"Yeah, I'd kind of figured that." Looked like some of the more outlandish rumours about him had been true after all—though he'd certainly done a pretty convincing vampire impression, that night in the bar when he'd attacked Mason.

Mason. I shuddered at the memory of Alberto's hand disappearing into his chest. No, definitely not a vampire. But then why pretend? Why spend all day in his cellar if he didn't have to?

"Then what are you?" Jake asked. "Some kind of airshaper?"

Could an airshaper do what he'd done with the billowing darkness?

"No. But that's not a bad idea. I could work with that."

I rolled my eyes. Fine. Whatever. If he didn't want to tell us, he didn't have to. I was beyond caring.

"Alberto, thanks for saving us. I'm really grateful, but it's been a rough couple of days, and if I don't get to bed soon I'm going to lay right down here in the street and go to sleep." I leaned in and kissed his smooth cheek, suddenly unutterably weary. "I don't care what you are. Or who. Do I still call you Alberto?"

"You can call me whatever you like. But my real name's Hades."

My head spun. Surely he didn't mean—? "As in, Hades, the god of the underworld? *That* Hades?"

I guess that would explain a few things. It certainly seemed to settle the question of whether or not the gods were real.

"The very same." He grinned. "At your service."

THE END

Don't miss the next book, *Murdered Gods*, coming soon! For news on its release, plus special deals and other book news, sign up for my newsletter at www.marinafinlayson.com.

Reviews and word of mouth are vital for any author's success. If you enjoyed *Stolen Magic*, please take a moment to leave a short review where you bought it. Just a few words sharing your thoughts on the book would be extremely helpful in spreading the word to other readers (and this author would be immensely grateful!).

ALSO BY MARINA FINLAYSON

MAGIC'S RETURN SERIES

The Fairytale Curse

The Cauldron's Gift

THE PROVING SERIES

Moonborn

Twiceborn

The Twiceborn Queen

Twiceborn Endgame

SHADOWS OF THE IMMORTALS SERIES

Stolen Magic

Murdered Gods (coming soon)

ACKNOWLEDGEMENTS

Thanks once again to my usual beta reading crew, Chris, Geoff, Mal and Alana, for your help with catching my oopses and your general support. Special thanks also to Rick Gualtieri for his awesome feedback and to my accidental alpha reader, Connor.

ABOUT THE AUTHOR

Marina Finlayson is a reformed wedding organist who now writes fantasy. She is married and shares her Sydney home with three kids, a large collection of dragon statues and one very stupid dog with a death wish.

Her idea of heaven is lying in the bath with a cup of tea and a good book until she goes wrinkly.